MW00427541

The Pact
Book I

Robert Patrick Lewis

Copyright © 2014 3 Pillars Enterprises, Inc

All rights reserved.

ISBN: 978-0-9859404-6-1

DEDICATION

<u>To my friends and family:</u> As I sit here, contemplating the time spent writing this I'm reminded of just how rough my life has been during its writing. Thank you for standing by me when I needed you most. I'm forever grateful and this would have never been finished if not for your undying support.

<u>Natalie:</u> When one door closes, another opens. You came into my life when I was at my worst; heartbroken, alone, and not knowing which way was up. You picked me up, brought me back to life, showed me what a truly supportive relationship really is and allowed me to see what my best looks like. You spoil me rotten and hold me to task at the same time, and my children and I are eternally grateful. Thank you baby, I love you.

<u>To Tactical 16 Publishing, Vets On Media and The Military Media Mafia Family:</u> I've heard countless stories of authors and their publishers getting into historic disagreements over missed deadlines or books changing from their original story. As with any good story, the one unfolded in the following pages has missed deadlines due to my own personal circumstances over the past year. The story has changed several times and the characters, well, they took on a life of their own. Rather than getting mad and drawing a line in the sand, all of those above simply asked what they could do to help me in my time of need and told me to make this book however it was meant to be, whenever it was meant to be. I cannot express how grateful I am for that, and I hope the way this story has come along is testament in itself to those choices you made to let it come to life.

<u>To the men of 022, The Regiment, Special Operations and Veterans:</u> This is my first fiction work, but as those close to me know, it is written in the context of current events that keep me up late at night in worry for what we have fought for. Stay vigilant, my Brothers, and remember the oath that we all took to defend this country and her constitution.

To my Brethren of Los Angeles Lodge #42, The Los Angeles Valley of the Scottish Rite and Sir Knight Brother Robert Johnson: I once wrote an article for the Midnight Freemasons about how conspiracy theories brought me into Masonry, but the brotherly love, support and virtues are what kept me there. Masonry came into my life when I needed it most, and each of you has paid true testament to the fraternity through your just and true actions.
  Thank you for being there when I needed a shoulder, a rock and a place to call home. Thank you, Brother Robert Johnson, for helping me with the Masonic intricacies and late-night, last-minute phone calls to make sure I had everything just right for this book. I hope this story reflects well and shows the true esteem in which I hold The Order.

VIRTUS JUNXIT MORS NON SEPARABIT

De Oppresso Liber

Nous Defions

God Bless America

CONTENTS

ACKNOWLEDGMENTS

Editing: Page by Page Editing
Cover Design: Bryan Dolch

INTRODUCTION
ZERO HOUR

I still remember the moment I realized Zero Hour was upon us.

The hospital had a full schedule of surgeries booked that day and it looked as if we were going to have another late night. I finished my residency a few years previously, so I still sat pretty low on the totem pole as far as scheduling was concerned.

Everything changed during my second case of the morning when I was sewing the patient up. I had asked the nurses to play internet radio while I was performing surgery to keep the mood light and the day progressing.

In the middle of one of my favorite songs, a rather fast-paced Texas country music tune by Mike Amabile and Run Over Twice that I had really been getting into, the Internet feed abruptly cut and the music stopped. The silence echoed loudly in the sterile OR, so I asked the nurse to refresh the browser.

When her answer came back that the Internet was out, my heart skipped a beat. Being in one of the top hospitals in the world - one so big it had a power station of its own - it was not likely our internet connection would just happen to go down.

I asked the nurse to check the operating room phone which was connected to a new VoIP network, backed up to prevent it from going down in an emergency. When she reported the phone network was also out I began to back away from the patient, told my residents to finish closing, and made my way for the desk.

Checking my cell phone was the last test.

Taking a glance and seeing that network down as well, I knew what had to happen next. I instructed the residents to close, grabbed the bag from my locker, headed to my truck without even changing out of my scrubs, and pulled my satellite phone out as soon as I left the garage.

I knew we didn't have much time. I immediately called home and when my children's nanny picked up, I said, "Start loading the tough boxes into the Defender."

"What?"

"It's time to go."

"What?"

"It's happening," I said, as calmly as I could. "We need to get out of Los Angeles now and head for Colorado. I'll be home as soon as I can. Get the kids ready. I don't know how long we have until it's too late."

"Ok, hurry, and please be careful!" she replied with fear and trepidation in her voice.

We had been through this drill at a minimum of every month for several years, but this was real and I could tell from her voice she was terrified.

"Get my guns out, they're loaded and ready to rock. Don't go anywhere without them until I get home. Do exactly what we planned. If you start seeing soldiers before I arrive, go into the mountains and I'll find you."

Once I heard her hang up, I said a silent prayer. *Please let my family still be alive when I get there.* Pushing the accelerator as far as it would go, I passed 100mph as I raced along I-10 East toward our house in the San Bernardino mountains outside of Los Angeles.

It was still early enough that I didn't encounter much traffic and was home within half an hour. Pulling into my driveway, I could see the nanny in the driveway, dragging the large tough boxes loaded with our supplies out of the garage and next to my Land Rover Defender.

We had been through this drill before and I paid her quite well to be ready for this exact situation.

2

With no time for pleasantries, I gave the kids a quick kiss, ran upstairs to change and appeared back in the garage carrying the rest of my guns and tactical gear.

"Go get all of the food you can fit into a cooler. We hit the road in less than ten minutes."

Without a word she headed back into the house and to the kitchen. We had enough canned and dehydrated food in the big black tough boxes to last us at least a year, but with two young children it was best to err on the side of caution.

With the last box loaded into the truck, I pulled a large, sealed envelope out of my backpack.

Each member of my old Special Forces Operational Detachment - Alpha [ODA], along with a few others - had their own version which we all hoped we would never have to open.

I fished through the contents until I found the packet labeled "Lewis" and pulled it out. Inside awaited a highly-detailed map set with satellite imagery and waypoints all the way from Los Angeles to Colorado Springs, letting our guys know which route we would be taking, where we would be stopping to rest, and where to find us if we didn't make it within the next 36 hours.

There was a list of protocols we created which would let us know our plan needed to be set into motion. A few different chains of events would trigger them, like natural disasters or social unrest.

The day's chain of events let us see the unthinkable was about to happen: the phone network going down, the internet network going offline, and the power grid being lost.

As if to answer any doubts left in my mind, I saw our garage lights shut off as the nanny walked back out from the kitchen carrying a cooler, letting me know we were out of time.

Everyone was packed up and in the car in a matter of moments. As I set the fuses for our booby traps and manually pulled down the garage door, I prayed silently that this was all a coincidence and I was dreadfully wrong.

The gates to our subdivision had been open when the power went out, and as we said goodbye to the nanny and our idyllic gated mountain community, I saw what I had feared was coming from the second the internet radio went out: paratroopers falling from the sky over downtown Los Angeles, and the planes they were jumping from were not ours

CHAPTER 1

DON'T LOOK BACK

As we drove along the mountains toward the Nevada border, my mind raced, trying to figure out who comprised the enemy forces and why they were invading us. I expected to find roadblocks in Barstow, but when they never materialized I figured the invaders hadn't been able to advance that far inland quite yet.

I tried to put my thoughts one step ahead, remembering our plans and operations for the Iraq and Afghanistan invasions, in which Special Forces landed on the ground long before the Marines and journalists showed up. If it were us, how would we stage this invasion, and who would be leading the attack?

That many of the world's leaders hated us was no great secret, even though their youth tried to emulate our culture as much as possible, and I guess it could only be a matter of time before someone worked up the courage to take a shot at the United States.

Most people believed the USA had never been invaded before, but in fact foreign enemy troops landed on American soil several times in the past, with German sabotage agents arriving in New York and Florida during World War II, Japanese soldiers landing in Alaska and multitudes of Russian spies finding their way here in the years of the cold war.

We had been well aware every country with a grudge against America infiltrated intelligence or terror cells within our borders while I was on active duty.

But as the American public had been a well-armed militia on our own due to the forward-thinking of our forefathers and nation's founders creating the second amendment, every one of our enemies knew an attack on mainland America would have made the partisan fighting in Iraq seem like child's play.

Only two terms of America's most naive and liberal presidents in its entire history were needed to disarm the law-abiding sheep of the public. Once the people found themselves unarmed, our military had been stretched thin at home and abroad, and our economy was on the downturn, the global chess pieces found themselves all in place.

That explained the why, but what about the who and how? Paying close attention to the world news, I had become increasingly worried when I saw the alliances our enemies were making with each other - especially Iran, Russia, China and North Korea.

But how?

I thought back to the Iraq invasion, to the stories of how our guys drove eighteen-wheelers full of guns, money and supplies through several countries and into Northern Iraq. Mexico had become nothing short of lawless in the past decade as the drug cartels seized all of the major shipping routes of the country, and I didn't think they'd bat an eye to accept payment from one of our enemies to help them get whatever they needed across the border.

I had been out of the Army for quite some time and remembered constant TS-Level reports coming through when I was active about the Battalion-sized elements of Chinese and Russian nationals who spent their days trying to find ways to hack into our power grid.

It wasn't too much of a stretch that they finally found a way in during the five years I had been a civilian. Everything began to make perfect sense as I white-knuckled the steering wheel, looking in my rear view mirrors every half-mile for the enemy.

Our route took us through a set of four phase lines on the way to Colorado, each with a nine-hour time window, starting from Zero Hour. Calling Ray on the satellite phone started the clock and every nine hours from that second, both groups would, hopefully, progress to another phase line.

Our compound in Colorado was the last point, so they were given nine hours to assemble the team and get ready to move. At nine hours and one minute, they would start off for the next phase line and would continue forward along my routes until we met or they arrived at my house, our starting location.

I left the signal of an orange piece of cloth inside my mailbox so the team - upon arriving at my house and finding that marker - would know that my family and I were out of town and started our journey eastward.

The idea was for us to get away from as many large cities as possible in the first twelve hours, and Las Vegas had been my goal. Our first phase line put us just on the other side of the city, at a spot on the lake in the Valley of Fire State Park.

I knew if we could make it that far we would be on smooth ground, as the beginning of the assault would be focused on major cities where they would "shock and awe" us and try to gain a psychological advantage.

A valuable lesson every Green Beret learns in Robin Sage, SERE, and the various Intelligence schools is if you want any chance to escape or take the upper hand in a kidnapping/ambush/attack, it has to be in the beginning - before your enemy has time to settle in and make plans.

Chaos was horrible for them, but perfect for people like us who could keep calm and organize while the rest of the world was on fire.

Chaos was what we did, what we were made of, and where guys like us felt most comfortable.

As I pulled off the highway and up to our designated home for the night, I sensed an immense wave of gratitude wash over me. I played the situation over time and time again in my head ever since I sat around the table with the team creating the map, and none of the scenarios we planned anticipated me making it all the way to our first stop without any resistance.

I found a good spot to park the truck on the other side of the mountain range, putting its elevation between the highway and us in case any enemy happened to pass by.

For all intents and purposes, the site was as good as we were going to get: the location of a huge lake a few minutes walk south and the mountain I was at the base of gave me enough elevation to view Las Vegas and any unwanted company.

The natural features of the mountain range and lake gave us a perfect choke point should I have to defend in place, so I was set.

By the time the kids finished eating their sandwiches, the tent had been constructed and sleeping bags were ready.

Avery was only two years old and Robert four, so neither of them possessed the maturity or powers of observation to be afraid. I put them to bed before setting in our camouflage and hiding our presence.

I had a long night in store for me, but I knew sleep would be something I wouldn't get much of until this all ended, and if I didn't get my priorities of work done first, we might not see the morning.

With the kids asleep and our tracks covered, I started my climb up the mountain.

My mind began to wander and be thankful I had the forethought to plan for this, packing away dehydrated food and MREs, buying and making extra ammo and constantly cleaning and oiling up my guns, even burying them in our backyard rather than turn them in when the California Gestapo-government came to take them away from the law-abiding citizens.

My ex-wife expended countless hours toiling on about the idiocy and worthlessness of our plan and the money I spent on emergency preparation, always wanting to spend our savings on expensive dinners or fancy cars, never quite understanding what had me so afraid.

Most people would never understand what I was planning for, why I was always so cheap with material things, yet quick to buy the highest-rated camping and survival gear, which weren't inexpensive by any means.

But I had been in enough combat zones and on enough missions to know there may come a time when they would be needed, and the middle of an emergency is the worst time to plan.

I was half way up the mountain, reliving my recent past and thanking God for keeping me dedicated to my preparations when the fireworks started.

With Las Vegas not too far to our west, I felt the earth tremble with the first bomb impact before I saw the flash. I hadn't climbed as high up as I intended, but wanted to get a good vantage point in case there would be anything to tip me off and prove me right on my assumptions as to what flag the enemy was fighting for.

I tried to keep my eyes fixed on the only pass someone could access to find my family sleeping below, but every few seconds the orange flames of a missile streak or anti-aircraft gun lighting up the sky from the Air Force bases outside of Las Vegas would grab my attention.

While the rockets, bombs and anti-aircraft rounds lit up the darkness, my thoughts became centered on the Land Rover Defender a few hundred feet below me. The fact we survived the day and made it out of the city was due to my Special Forces training and the pact which I made with my brothers, the family of men from my ODA for whom I felt the strongest love and tie that a group of men can possess for each other.

But in the truck below slept a different love and the reason I left instead of fighting in place - my family.

Robert, my oldest child, who at only four years old was smarter than any of his classmates and was proving to be a fine athletic specimen.

He exhibited all of the same features I showed from the pictures of my childhood. The only real physical trait he shared with his mother were her brown eyes in place of my hazel, and it was the perfect complement to his tan complexion, thick, chestnut-colored hair and a grin that would melt the ladies' hearts one day.

And of course there was Avery. I had always mocked the "daddy's little girl" idea, but the second I met her, I knew she had me wrapped around her finger.

Perhaps it was because she bore each of the gorgeous features of her mother: the fine, shiny black hair, perfectly round face, a big gummy smile at two years old that would knock anybody down, and to top it all off, my hazel eyes with the almond shape of her Asian characteristics.

As the fires in the sky lit up the night and the impact of their explosions shook the earth beneath me, I couldn't bring myself to sit still anymore. I would fight once I was reunited with my brothers, that much was true.

But for now my mission was to get my family to safety, far from this dark, Godless place full of fear and fire.

CHAPTER 2

BONA FIDES

I wasn't sure who won the battle that raged in the sky throughout the night, or if it even resulted in a clear winner.

When my watch struck five a.m. and the sun began to crest the horizon and illuminate the smoke still lingering from the barrage, I knew I had to get back down to the truck and start moving.

I suspected the bombardment had been nothing more than a show of force. Like the initial invasion phase in any military campaign, this was an attempt by the enemy to take out as many of our forces as possible and prove we weren't holding air superiority here like we utilized in the past few wars.

The rising sun began to light up tiny reflections off the pieces of wreckage from the planes our boys shot down, and I smiled a bit as I climbed back down to my family sleeping in the truck below, glad we weren't taking this invasion sitting down.

Our gear was packed up and ready to go before the sun was over the horizon, but I wanted to give the kids as much time to sleep as I could. I had lived this life; knew the wear and tear that combat and sleepless nights take on your mind and body.

But even though they were right in the middle of it, I wanted to keep them as sheltered from what I had experienced as much as possible.

I pulled my map out and silently went over our plans, visualizing the route in my head. The team picked this one after much deliberation, knowing my top priority would be to get out of Los Angeles and past Las Vegas as swiftly as was achievable. So far we were mission accomplished.

The terrain allowed at least a half-dozen routes to choose from, but only someone who's been in and around the invasions of other countries can give a real fact-based approach to planning how to escape one themselves.

We knew the first twelve hours would be absolute chaos. A military force couldn't just fly or sail all of their troops in without being picked up by radar, so it was safe to assume they would be coming in increments, and chaos would be used to mask the larger troop movements into our country.

In the same method we Green Berets utilized to invade Afghanistan and Iraq, this enemy would need to send in some sort of commandos first.

They would start by bringing in small groups with men and weapons to cause the first diversions and instituting guerilla warfare to keep us off-guard. That would allow the follow-on main forces of conventional troops to roll on in and set up bases.

We assumed it would take at least twenty-four hours for enough soldiers to land to even begin taking over large cities, so if I could get my family past Las Vegas before that window hit, we'd be in smooth sailing for the rest of the trip.

Throughout the next leg of our journey, I couldn't decide whether I should be terrified and constantly on the lookout for gunships and checkpoints, or relieved we made it this far inland and safely away from major metropolitan areas.

I tried to keep my eyes glued to the sky, but they continued to grow heavier with every passing minute and mile. As with everything in my life, I followed an ordered and deliberate fashion in my actions; eyes on the road, then to the surrounding Utah mountains, next to the sky.

Once my scan for the enemy was complete, I'd give myself a brief second to move my eyes to the rear view to watch Robert and Avery, keeping themselves entertained and busy with the educational DVDs and toys I packed.

I caught myself starting to doze on more than a few occasions. All commercial radio had either been knocked out or abandoned so I couldn't find any station with news, and didn't want to play any music lest I miss the soft whir of a helicopter or the crack of incoming rounds.

The only activities available to keep my mind busy were the constant inventorying of the boxes in our trunk and the items I shipped to our compound in Colorado, the continual thought of how tired I was and how great it would be to get some rest when we arrived at our destination.

This was by far the longest but most beautiful part of our trip, and I made frequent stops at gas stations to ensure all of our fuel cans and gas tank were topped off. Gas would be a supreme luxury now, as it should have been treated decades ago, along with water, food, and anything else our society had taken for granted.

Every time we would stop at a deserted station, I would let the kids expend some built up energy and stretch their legs. As I connected my portable Fill Rite fuel transfer pump to the stations' diesel tanks, I prayed I would be able to keep them from ever having to experience the horrors I witnessed during my time in war zones.

As a soldier in another country, you are forced to build up a wall of defenses lest you allow any of the inhumanity you witness on a daily basis get into your soul.

It was common to watch the expression on another soldier's face start off as excited but scared during the first part of a combat tour, then see that excitement and fear slowly turn to anger, pity, and a relentless awareness of inability to offer any help in the form that the innocent civilians needed most.

Watching Robert and Avery run around in circles like they were in the schoolyard on any given bright, sunny weekend brought back memories of the young children I would witness in Iraq and Afghanistan, playing soccer next to the burned out hulls of trucks and tanks destroyed in the heat of battle.

We came to the last stop of the day as the sun made its quick race for the horizon, ready to leave us in darkness to light up the rest of the world. I tried to burn the image of them playing in my mind, oblivious to what was going on and the childhood innocence I wished they would never have to lose.

I let them play until they found themselves panting and worn out, and took an extra long time to hug and kiss their foreheads as I put them back in the truck.

In less than twenty-four hours, my job as a father transitioned from working hard to provide them with the best schooling, food, and home to merely keeping them safe and alive, and I thanked God for my training and friends that would enable me to accomplish that.

As we pulled into our designated spot for the night, a wave of relief washed across me as I spied the first Bona Fides as soon as we exited off the road.

We planned that if it ever came to this, everyone would be on high-alert and heavily armed, so my Brothers and I set different levels of signals to identify ourselves and give each other a sign when we arrived at one of our link-up positions.

A casual passerby would have never noticed, but the blue Afghani scarf tied around a tree limb along a dirt road leading to a lake told me that our boys were waiting a little farther down to take us home.

Had anything happened to them upon their arrival, they would have died making sure that the scarf came down on their way out, just as I would have if it had been our sign to them.

As our protocol dictated, I stopped our truck and turned off the engine as I rounded the last corner. With the kids fast asleep in the back, I locked the doors and turned to head out of the door. I was barely to the hood when I heard Ray's voice.

"Berg," his voice rang out with his thick midwestern accent.

"Heil," I replied without missing a beat.

"What took you so damn long?" he asked as several dark figures began to move toward me.

"You know how LA is. Traffic was a son of a bitch," I answered as I walked forward to meet them.

I counted four shadows walking toward me and knew there would be at least two more hidden away in over-watch positions somewhere; snipers with a trained eye on the road to give us a fair warning if unexpected company was inbound.

Matty was the first face I recognized through the darkness, and he dropped his rifle to the side as he walked up and gave me a big bear hug.

"Good to see you, Brother."

"You too. How's Kristen?"

"She's back at the compound with the others. The kids?"

"In the truck, sleeping."

"When was the last time you slept?"

"Doesn't matter, I'll sleep when we get home."

"Bullshit," Chris chimed in from behind Matty.

"Our time window is closing pretty fast, so we'll need everyone on their A-game for this last leg of the trip. Their night vision technology is better than ours, so we might as well get a little shut-eye while we can and move once the sun comes up."

Knowing it was an exercise in futility to argue with Chris, my body finally allowed me to let my guard down now that the guys were there to guard over my family. Sensing the absolute exhaustion in my bones, I knew I couldn't have made it much farther anyway.

Chris knew me better than anyone ever could, and he saw it in my eyes that I needed to rest. So before I could pass any more bravado, he gave me his marching orders.

"J-Lo and Klint are up top on overwatch. We'll replace them throughout the night. You get your butt back in that truck with your family and grab some shut-eye. We'll get you when it's time to go."

Not having the words to express how grateful I felt they were actually there nor the energy to say them even if I did, all I could do was hold out my closed fist.

Chris nodded, winked and gave me a fist bump, a much deeper communication than most guys would get from hours of talking.

The next thing I knew, J-Lo was gently nudging my shoulder to wake me up. As soon as he saw the recognition in my eyes, he gave me the ten-minutes-till-roll-out hand gesture, signaling to me we were getting ready to leave.

I looked back at Robert and Avery asleep in sleeping bags that were laid out on the backbenches of the Defender, sleeping as soundly as if they were tucked into their own beds back at home.

The guys were ready to roll long before us, and seeing them loaded in the trucks, weapons at the ready and ammo bulging out of every available inch of space brought back some fond memories of our time downrange together.

People have a difficult time understanding exactly what makes a Special Forces team such a force to be reckoned with, but it's much more simple than one would imagine.

Sure, we're all a bit smarter, tougher, stronger, and better shots than the average bear. We've been through years of the hardest and best training any military in the world could possibly come up with. We've been tested for years on end to prove we are the best of the best and never miss a step.

But none of that even scratches the surface.

At the end of the day, we are loyal. Athletes and many others in popular society like to use the word "Brother" as a term of endearment, and there is no such thing as a friend in Special Forces. An ODA truly is a small family, and the bonds of Brotherhood are much stronger than any words could ever explain.

Any ODA will form these bonds, but when you have an ODA like ours, which had been deployed together to many different theaters of combat and who had saved each other's lives on more than one occasion, the loyalty we possess for each other is as much a part of our lives as breathing.

We were over an hour into the drive when my radio chirped to life, jolting me out of my daydream and romanticized memories of our various exploits together.

"We got incoming," Ray warned through the radio.

"It looks like gunships, three of them about ten miles out, following the road and coming in from our northeast."

"Get the hell off the road, everyone! Pull off to the right here - we'll take cover in the mountains," came Chris' order.

The job of an 18C on a Special Forces ODA is that of an engineer, and while their black-and-white job description sounds pretty fun (building and blowing stuff up), they have one of the most integral jobs on an ODA: procurement.

Ray and Chris had taken this job very seriously and had earned quite the reputation for their sticky fingers and ability to barter for anything under the sun when it was needed.

Ray's dad had been a Green Beret in the Vietnam days and it seemed those unwritten but most important of jobs were passed along in the family because Ray was exceptional when it came to the art of procurement.

I'm not sure how in the world he went about it, but somewhere along the line, Ray managed to procure a Blue Force Tracker.

This was a radar of sorts outfitted in our trucks downrange which had GPS and map overlays, and also gave us the ability to pick up any other vehicles with GPS (like enemy trucks or helicopters) and show them on the map in respect to our trucks.

I followed as the convoy hurriedly pulled off the road and Ray came over the radio again.

"We got about two minutes. Better make it quick, guys."

"Shut off your radios and any electronics you have," added Chris.

As the vehicles came to a stop about a hundred feet off the road, the guys jumped out with camouflaged netting to throw over the tops. J-Lo sprinted from the front truck back to ours and threw the corner of a net to me as we covered my Defender.

Just as I started to unroll my end of the netting, I sensed something that made the hair on the back of my neck stand up. I began to feel the bass and vibrations in the ground and off of the surrounding mountains before I heard anything, but I had been on the giving end of enough helicopter-infiltration missions to know what was coming.

J-Lo shot a quick worried glance at me as we pulled the last corner down and jumped in the Defender.

I looked back at the kids to make sure they were ok and found them both still asleep. I held my rifle close and squeezed my pouches to make sure I had plenty of ammo on me - not that it would do any good if the gunships spotted us.

I could feel them getting closer as the dull vibrations of the ground turned into shaking of the truck floor, and the reverberation off the mountains became a deafening cacophony of the unmistakable sound of the helicopter rotors. Just when I could tell they were right over us, I saw movement in the back seat and heard a cry.

I jumped into the back and covered my waking son with my body and a blanket, doing my best to keep him quiet. I nervously thumbed the selector switch on my AR-15, prepared to jump out of the truck and do what little I could if I heard the helicopters begin to circle around.

In truth, it would be like attempting to bring down an elephant with nothing more than rocks and sticks. But if this was going to be my end, I was going to make damn sure that I died in a pile of brass from expended ammo.

I switched my gaze from a tiny spot on my dashboard, trying to drown out everything aside from the dull thud of the rotor backwash against the roof of my Defender, with the reflection of J-Lo in the rearview mirror, eyes closed, knowing if we were spotted we'd be nothing more than bloody puddles at the push of the button in the gunships above us.

It wouldn't do us any good, but I hoped for a split-second head start if I detected the slightest change in the sound as the helicopters made the switch from forward progress to hover, or turned their ailerons and begun to spin back around toward us, because at least I could get a few shots off and go down fighting, hopefully taking out a pilot or navigator in the process as a final act of defiance.

But as the dull thud of the backwash rapidly became softer and softer and I felt the metal of my truck stop vibrating with each concussion, and I was partially relieved to hear the enemy moving farther and farther away, but a distinct part of me was disappointed.

I've struggled with the idea of religion my entire life, raised in the Episcopal and Baptist churches, losing all faith in religion after several combat deployments, and then marrying my ex-wife, a Buddhist, and coming into contact with the Dalai Lama & Karmapa. Countless late-night conversations with our friend Geshe-la, a high Buddhist monk, brought an entirely new perspective to my idea of life and faith.

I never went full-force into all of the Buddhist philosophy, but the belief of reincarnation and the continuation of souls and energy struck a familiar chord with me, especially after my experiences in Special Forces and with the guys that surrounded me now.

I had taken on the belief that certain souls are put into creation for a specific purpose in the world, such as the Dalai Lama and the Buddhist Rinpoches who are believed to be reincarnations meant to strive for the final attainment of enlightenment. While they are meant to help the world by promoting peace and oneness, I thought, guys like me sat at the opposite end of the spectrum.

Rather than devoting our lives to the ultimate attainment of peace through nonviolence and passivity, souls like ours were put into the universe to be sheepdogs.

Warriors.

Those devoted to fighting for good and protecting those who couldn't protect themselves; the soldiers of the Light in the ultimate battle with those whose souls and agendas were nothing but darkness.

I wasn't sure how much time passed before Ray lifted the netting over my window and gave me the signal to roll out, but it seemed like an eternity.

J-Lo shot me a quick and knowing look, one that communicated the fact we had always known there must be a lucky horseshoe hidden up one of our backsides.

But luck wouldn't be enough to get us through too many more close calls like that.

Without a word, he put his gloved fist up for a fist-bump, and after the tap, made his way out of my truck to retake his spot up front.

I couldn't stop looking around as we pulled out, craning my neck like the father driving on a family vacation looking for a landmark to show everyone, still not believing they flew right over us and gone on their way without a second glance.

I continued on like that for hundreds of miles and during the multiple rest stops we had to take in order for Robert and Avery to relieve themselves.

Two of the first things which become well-trained in Special Forces are your bladder and nature calls, but unfortunately that training isn't hereditary, and as my kids still didn't understand what was going on, we were stopping every hundred miles or so.

Back in the convoy and on the road, my mind began to wander. For the first time since my internet went out in the OR, I had the only guys I trusted in the world keeping a lookout for my family now and I couldn't help but wonder what came next.

We had gone over these plans many times before, but always under the "what if" assumption, and always after more than a few drinks.

This was as real as it got, and while the awake, sober father in me dreaded what came next, there was another deeper, hidden part of me - the warrior-soul I thought had been left on the battlefields in the desert - that was excited.

CHAPTER 3

DEFEND IN PLACE

My mind had grown completely numb from the road by the time I started seeing the familiar rise and fall of the Cheyenne mountain range.

I half expected there to be a smoking crater where the mountain itself used to sit, being that it was public knowledge the old NORAD [North American Aerospace Defense Command] Headquarters was once buried deep within the rock.

That would have been an opportune target for a first strike, but for some reason it seemed the enemy hadn't even tried, as the site contained none of the telltale signs of exploded ordinance or smoking craters.

When Ray hatched this plan and we all signed on, we took the money we each squirreled away from years spent apart from our families in the deserts and dirt holes of the world and bought a pretty sizable piece of property outside of The Springs in a perfectly defensible area.

The compound was situated on high ground and outfitted with our own water supply, and while Ray lived on and took care of the land, we each took our turns visiting and doing our part to make improvements and keep the place in tip-top shape.

It was a bit of a drive once we passed The Springs, but when we started driving along the ever-familiar long, dirt road leading to our gate and huge metal cattle fencing that would stop a Mack truck at full speed, I knew we were finally safe.

The wives stood outside and began running towards the trucks, smiling and waving before we even stopped, and as soon as Robert saw Ray's wife, Sarah, he let out an excited squeal.

We hadn't been able to see each other too often once I left the Army and started my journey onto med school to become a doctor, but these guys always remained closer to me than family, and we made sure our kids grew up together, with the parental advice of our entire village.

I got out for a little stretch, and seeing Jason's wife, Deanna, heading right for me, I smiled and opened my arms for a hug just as she pushed past to get to the children.

"Come on, Rob, you know where my priorities are," she laughed.

As tight and close as we guys were, I found it amazing how much closer our families had always been. They say an ODA maintains its own personality, and if yours doesn't fit it'll suck to be you. It only made sense the women who spent so long putting up with us would be a special breed themselves.

I took a quick look around while the ladies and kids got reacquainted. At least a year had passed since I was able to do my time helping out and I noticed quite a few upgrades were made in my absence.

The walls, fence and gates were reinforced several times over, and as I walked around the compound I found the doors to half a dozen of our underground storage facilities open. Outside the doors stood large piles of ammo, food and supplies stacked on the ground and in the process of being moved in.

I made my way over to the guys who were circled around the lead truck, hacking out plans for the near future as far as I could tell. Ray got a big smirk on his face as I walked towards them, held out his arms and made one of his typically loud, smart-ass comments, meant more to take a jab at me than to convey any information.

"Whaddaya think, doc? I know you've been busy in Los Angeles saving people and all, but we've been working pretty hard out here while you spent your days drinking martinis and smoking cigars with your pansy doctor friends," he said.

I smiled and admired the accommodations, nodding at the obvious improvements I noticed previously.

"Yeah, Ray, looks like you've been pretty busy here. But when you get a splinter in that dainty little finger of yours, you'll be thankful for all those cigar and martini hours I logged!"

"Take it to the team house everyone," yelled Chris, obviously fresh out of patience for horsing around.

"We've got a lot to go over."

Without a word or hesitation, we began to move towards the team house, our own little base of operations situated behind the main house.

I shot a glance at Deanna on my way to make sure she knew where I was going, and her nod told me she was on the same page.

Everything would be different from now on, but I hoped deep down in my heart that, if anything at all, my relationship with the kids didn't change any more than it had to.

The first thing I observed when I walked in was a huge map hung up on the far wall, and as I moved past a HAM radio, weapons, ammo, various planning documents and papers full of red ink, I took a seat against the wall. Chris made his way to the front of the room to give us our orders.

"First I want to say welcome back, Rob. It's good to have you back, Brother," he said.

"Thanks for actually coming to get me guys!" I replied, half joking, but feeling the full force and truth of gratitude inside my soul.

"We've got a lot to do, so there isn't any time to screw around," he continued. "There are three more convoys that should be arriving sometime in the next forty-eight hours, and I'd like to ensure everyone's beds and the base security is ready by the time they get here. Everyone knows their implied tasks, right?"

Looking around the room, Chris found all heads nodding up in down in affirmation. As part of an ODA, each man has an "implied task" based on his job, a basic set of duties nobody should ever need to tell him to do; it's just our place to always make sure it's kept up and finished - no matter what else is going on.

Being both a doctor and the team's former medic, I had been writing prescriptions and stockpiling all the antibiotics and supplies I could over the past few years so that our pharmacy and medical center remained updated, should the need ever arise.

My implied task was to always make sure our meds stayed up-to-date, to treat anyone who needed it, to keep the team trained in trauma management and basic medical skills, and to make sure our sanitation and hygiene protocols were always in good order.

And as the guy with the most biology, chemistry, and green-thumb experience, I was unofficially one of the guys in charge of the greenhouse.

At least I wouldn't be alone. Jason, Corey, Klint and Adam were other medics who had been brought in on the plan, and as Adam had been working for a biotechnology firm specializing in plant and food technology, he'd be the lead on the greenhouse.

J-Lo, Josh and Tattoo were in charge of the weapons and security plan for the whole compound.

Ray, Chris, Buckeye and Tony would be in charge of "procurement"; we'd give them lists of things we needed and they'd figure out ways to go about getting them. The four of them were also responsible for the physical upkeep and building around the compound, as they encompassed all the engineering experience on the team.

And, of course, their favorite job - which would come in handy now - of making as many improvised bombs and explosive devices as they could.

As our former communications guys, Matty, Chad and Griz would take the reins on all our communication - with each other, listening to the enemy, and trying to contact other fighting forces.

The HAM radio in the corner was their baby, and as I had seen them make working radios out of beer cans and batteries, I was pretty interested to see what they would come up with for us.

After seeing all heads nodding in accordance, Chris gave his next directive.

"Ray, show Rob's family to their room. Rob, take a few minutes to explain what's going on to your kids and then get to work."

"What's our plan?" I asked. "I mean, after the other guys get here, when do we start?"

I could tell by the expressions in the room everyone had been asking themselves the same question. A Green Beret's primary training and job in war is unconventional warfare (sometimes referred to as Guerrilla Warfare), and while we had conducted UW on many other battlefields before, this time it was on our turf and we were chomping at the bit to get started.

"Soon, Brother," he replied. "We'll start taking it to them soon, but first we have to get everyone here and get organized. We don't want to strike too early or give away our location. We'll wait for Bulldog and Josh to get here so we can start planning and do this the smart way. We made it this far, no sense rushing and getting ourselves and our families killed now."

That was an excellent point. If we were going to launch random attacks, there was no reason to re-group like this and painstakingly make all the plans we spent years working on. Unconventional warfare is an art and as masters of chaos, nobody knew how to paint that masterpiece better than an ODA.

It wasn't our task to try and take whoever the enemy was head-on as that would be nothing more than suicide. Our team was just over a dozen men and without proper planning, our true talents would go to waste.

Our job was to hit them behind their own lines, to make their life difficult, and lower their morale so much that they imploded. This needed to be done intelligently, which meant taking the time to choose and plan our targets of opportunity.

Turning to the map, Chris pointed out several points marked in red, spread all across the country. Seeing one based in Los Angeles with our phase lines to Colorado all marked, I knew what it was for.

"We have these three convoys on the way in, so we need to be prepared to receive them when they start arriving," Chris said.

"Rob, you will have today off QRF [Quick Reaction Force, an element always on standby to react if anyone on mission got into trouble] to get your own family situated, but everyone else has to be ready to move at any second if we get a distress call or these guys don't show up by their last hit time."

After our initial brief, Ray followed me out to the trucks to get my kids and led us to our room. As a safety precaution, we decided to put all the rooms underground in our own little fallout shelter and built an aboveground house not too far away as a sort of decoy. The idea was that anyone trying to launch an attack against us would strike there first, giving us at least a small heads-up.

It had taken us years to get everything to this point, but walking through the halls of our underground compound, I was still impressed.

Our first plans left the ceilings a little low for my taste, but Buckeye figured out a way to take shipping containers and cut the ends off for the hallways, giving us a solid foundation and high ceilings. Some reinforced concrete via Ray and we had ourselves a safe little place to call home.

I read up on sanitation for fallout shelters during our planning, and along with the engineers, came up with a pretty ingenious system for sewage and collecting rainwater, complete with our own little fish farm and filtration system. I heard Ray even found a way to add a solar-powered hydroponics system for vegetables and I wanted to poke around to explore everything as soon as we got settled in.

There were solar panels and wind turbines scattered all over our land, and combined with the hydroelectric power coming in via the river passing through our property, it gave us a pretty good amount of electricity. As I walked along the well-lit hallways, I was awestruck with all the improvements made over the last year since I'd been there to visit and pitch in.

We passed through several shipping containers worth of hallways, with perpendicular arms sprouting off on both sides in the middle of each. I recognized the four bathrooms we spent so much time and money to make just right, the UV greenhouse, the fish farm, the planning cell, the entertainment room, and then we started coming to the living quarters.

I hadn't been present for the building of any of these beyond the digging and pouring of concrete, so I was excited to play around and find what the guys had come up with. Ray stopped outside of the third living quarter on the right and held out his arm.

"Welcome to Chez Lewis, sir," he said. "Would you like me to turn down your pillow for you?"

Not quite getting the joke or sarcasm, Robert turned and gazed up at me with a puzzled look on his face.

"What's a chez, dad?"

"It means home in French, bud."
"But this isn't our home, dad," he replied.
I shot a glance at Ray, not knowing how to respond.
"It is for now, buddy," I replied. "This is our home for now."

CHAPTER 4

FIND, FIX AND DESTROY

The alarm clock's blaring sound woke me up from a deep slumber and illuminated our room with a faint blue light. I heard Robert begin to stir around, but it was still so early and our elevation so much higher than Los Angeles that he'd be sleeping for at least another few hours.

I put my feet on the cold ground and gazed around to size up the situation. With no sunlight or windows for it to come through, the morning fog in my head took me a few minutes to make absolutely certain this wasn't just a bad dream.

We each sacrificed time and money, and put up with quite a bit of complaining from our wives for this "grown up kids fort" they always saw as a monumental waste.

Now, this was turning out to be the best investment any of us ever made. I felt thankful this was a good group of guys who cared enough about our families to do this in the off-chance our worst nightmares ever became a reality as they had a few days ago.

Looking around our room, I marveled at how it was meticulously built with detail and craftsmanship. There were homemade bunks on each side, allowing Robert, Avery and I to have a bed of our own. Beyond the beds were built-in shelves, a few cubbyholes, a bookshelf and a desk for the kids.

Over the past few years, I sent medical books along with my supplies and somebody had been thoughtful enough to place them ready for use and stacked on my shelves.

As I began to lace up my boots, Robert sat up in bed and looked at me.

"Dad, why are we underground?"

"That's a good question, buddy."

"Are we hiding?"

"Yes, son. There are bad people here now. If they find the house above us, they won't think anything of it. But if they see a compound big enough for all of these people, they'd come to get us and take you kids away."

"Oh. I like it here."

"Good, buddy, I'm glad. Get some rest. It's going to be a long day and you'll need your energy."

"OK, Dad, I wuv you."

"I love you too, buddy."

I kissed him on the forehead and walked out of the room, closing the door as quietly as possible and contemplating my list of priorities. My first stop had to be the medical center which I helped design during the planning phase.

Though I had been sending supplies since we began building it, I hadn't stepped foot inside in over a year and needed to commit every inch to memory should an emergency arise. It was designed to handle several traumas at the same time, an absolute necessity in a war zone.

Having enough experience between us medics to make a seasoned ER doc in the busiest level one trauma center seem like a newbie, this one was organized more efficiently than any I had ever seen.

Walking into the converted ship container, I stopped, blown away at how well the guys had set it up. It was clear the other medics had spent quite a bit of time in there while I had been away.

One of the benefits of a Special Forces medic is access to medical equipment, most notably trauma gear that isn't available to the public yet.

Some call us the lab rats of trauma, beta testing the latest and greatest trauma technology before anything goes to market. I couldn't count the scores of lives our access to that equipment saved, and our suggestions would always result in modifications from the manufacturer within weeks.

Looking around the room, my eyes caught quite a few pieces of gear I had never seen before. I worked in one of the world's top hospitals, but being on the civilian side now meant waiting for these guys to test everything before I got my access, so I toyed with them a bit and made mental notes about what to ask.

It was still well before six in the morning, but I figured I'd go up top to investigate if anyone else was stirring. As I began to walk down the long hallway towards the stairs, a radio chirped to life from one of the rooms with a familiar voice on the other end.

"Eagles nest, this is zero-two-two-delta-one, twenty mics, over."

As I walked closer to investigate, Ray's voice replied, "Roger, delta-one. Welcome home."

I rounded the corner to find Ray in the communications room. I shot him a wide grin and asked, "Jason's coming back?"

"Yup! They went to get Adam the same time we left to get you guys, but they had quite a bit farther to go."

"Have you heard anything back from them before this?" I asked.

"They gave us a satellite call when they linked up, but we're trying to keep those as short and sweet as possible," he said. "No telling how long it will be before the enemy gains access to our satellites and numbers."

"Is there any news about what's happening around the rest of the country? How's the East Coast holding up? Anybody fighting back?"

"We know just about as much as you right now. We're still in the initial invasion phase, so it doesn't seem like anyone has had a chance to make sense of anything, or even get the HAM radio network up and running."

"Any idea what the plan is?"

"Take our country back, Brother. As soon as everyone's here, we start to do what we do best: find, fix and destroy the enemy."

Without much else to say, I headed upstairs to meet the team coming in. There were several convoys still out, and I was giddy with excitement to discover who this group would bring. I hadn't seen the guys in quite some time and every smiling face became a mini-reunion.

"What a weird way to have a reunion. Why couldn't we just get together to drink beer and play golf like normal friends?" I thought.

Once I arrived up top, I began to get things ready for the guys. I still had a little time, so I opted to open the garage first. Our whole reason for building the majority of the complex underground was to keep our numbers hidden, so it would defeat the purpose to leave all of our trucks parked in the driveway of a single four-bedroom house.

It was one distinct advantage of putting the minds of over a dozen guys with combat experience from all over the world together when planning something like this.

For example, we learned an important lesson from shoes in Iraq. The men wouldn't wear them inside, so if there were ever a question as to how many men we'd find in a house or building, we could typically move around the outside of the house, count the shoes and determine the number, size and age (kids vs adults) of people on the target.

We used that experience to decide if we were going to go "all in" and build this place right, doing everything possible to hide our total presence. With sixteen guys in our group, plus their associated wives and families, we would definitely raise some eyebrows with those numbers living on one compound, so we decided to go underground.

I was almost finished raising the doors to the subterranean garage with the manual hand crank when J-Lo called out.

"Eagles coming in."

I made one last rotation and turned in time to witness the first truck, a proper HUMVEE, complete with .50 cal on top, come through the gates with none other than Chad (aka Buckeye), my son's godfather, riding in the gunner's nest.

He shot me a grin and a quick wink as they drove through the doors and underground without so much as slowing down.

I watched and tried to get a glimpse of faces as the trucks rolled in, counting who hadn't arrived yet but not fully knowing what to expect.

Adam sped past with his family next, and Josh's bearded face shot me a big, toothy smile as the third truck drove in with Tattoo up top on the gun.

Two more medics and an integral part of our leadership had just come in, so I knew it was almost time to get started. I followed the last vehicle down into the garage, partly to ask if I could help, but mostly to share hugs all around with the Brothers I hadn't seen in far too long.

Buckeye was the first to jump down and wrap me up in a big bear hug. His first question came as no surprise.

"Where's the big guy?" he asked, eager to see his godson.

"He's downstairs, sleeping with Avery."

"How's he taking it?"

"I haven't had the time to sit them down and explain what's going on. Glad he didn't ask yet...I don't even know where to start."

"Brother, that kids sharper than any of us. I'll bet he knew what was going on before we did," he said.

Josh offered up a fist bump as he walked past, stopped and turned around as he began up the incline.

"Team room in ten minutes. Help Adam and his family carry their things, show them their room and get in there. Get the rest of the guys up. We've got some important news to go over!"

Just as with any time Josh spoke, we immediately heeded his word and got to action, each man going straight for Adam's truck and taking as much as he was able to carry.

It had been a long time since I had seen Adam and his family, so I gave his wife a hug and the kids each a head rub before meeting his fist bump and following it up with an embrace.

"Looking good there, Brother," I said.

"Thanks, Rob, you too."

"How was the trip?"

"Pretty hairy. I'll let Josh tell you about it," he replied.

He obviously didn't want to elaborate, and only then did I take notice of the shell-shocked expressions on his kids' faces. I had seen those looks countless times before on the faces of children in war zones, but not in quite a few years and I wasn't expecting to see it on them since our ride in had been relatively easy.

Knowing Adam was the right one to ease his children's minds, and there wasn't anything I could say or do, I gave him a slight nod, took a bag and tough box in my arms and started back to the rooms.

Adam was one of those guys with whom I maintained a close attachment from the first time we met. We were in the Q-course at the same time but never in the same part, and when we ended up at our first unit together, our friendship began as if we knew each other for years.

Special Forces medics are very particular in that we all follow closely defined life paths after graduating the Special Forces Qualification Course.

Like most SF guys, some 18Ds take on a role as a shooter and find their way to other organizations like Delta Force where they spend much of their time kicking down doors and exercising violence of action on the enemy.

But medics are selected for their brainpower, and many of us find our way towards intelligence courses during our time in SF. Those of us who find a real penchant for it usually find our way to other organizations that are only described by acronyms or code names - most of which the general public has never been told about.

The third path, one that Adam, Corey and I all shared was a profound love for medicine, none of us having ever realized that it existed within us before. Guys like us fight as hard as we can to stay on the teams as medics, and eventually find ourselves in med school or a physicians assistant program.

In Special Forces, no one is allowed to pick their own job; even if all you want to be is a weapons guy or a medic, and you have years of experience in either one of those areas, the final decision is made entirely by the Special Forces gods themselves and you are given no say in what your specialty ends up being.

Adam and I were total med nerds who would get together to compare notes and gear after work hours and on weekends in Germany, having as much fun procuring and stocking new med bags and equipment as the bravos did playing with new guns and sights.

I felt relieved to have him back. Not only was he tough as nails and better than the average shot (even the Special Forces average), but also a class-A medic. Corey, Adam, and Jason were the three best medics I've ever met, and with all of them back together with me at the compound, I knew that my family and everyone else there were in good hands.

A few minutes later, I entered the team room and sat in one of the office chairs around the table as Josh studied the map behind him.   It brought back fond memories of our time in Afghanistan to watch him stand in front of us, as he had many times before, stroking his beard, combing over a map and searching for the right way to communicate the thoughts encompassing his mind or our mission queue.

He started as soon as Adam entered through the doorway, closing the door behind him.

"Well that was a fun one, wasn't it, guys?" he asked.

I could tell by the smirk on his face and the muffled laughs around the room that more than a little sarcasm rested within his comment.

"For those of you who weren't with us, we got into a scuffle yesterday," he continued.

Looking around and seeing that everyone involved was waiting for him to clue us in, he pointed to the red flags on the map which represented the way points between our compound and Adam's house, smacking it loudly with the telescopic radio-antenna style pointer nestled in his hand.

"As soon as we got word from Adam they were headed this way, we rounded up two trucks and started moving. It seems as if the enemy realized a missile attack would trigger our algorithms to launch our own and end in mutually assured destruction, so from what we found, it looks as if they chose to sneak in quietly and take out our missile silos by hand because they were all over the Midwest."

"And the East Coast," Adam chimed in. "Given who it was, I'm not sure how they got onto the eastern seaboard so quickly, unless that's where they came in, but they were all over the place as soon as the first bombs started going off."

Something Adam said got my attention.

"Given who it was? You guys know who we're fighting here?" I asked.

He shot a glance at Josh and then around the room towards the rest of the group.

"Well, I can tell you that some of the guerrilla's I saw were Arabs," he said. "Didn't have enough time to investigate, but I witnessed more than a few groups of Arabs in plain clothes causing mayhem. Not looters - but trained dudes with a mission and purpose."

"What makes you say that?" I asked.

"I noticed it on my way in to work that morning. Arabs stick out in the Northeast, and I saw an awful lot of them on the way in to the city. I take the same route at the same time every day, so I found it strange that almost everywhere I looked there were Arabs who just, well, I don't know... didn't fit in."

"Didn't fit in how?" I pressed.

"I don't know, man...just didn't seem comfortable in their own skin," he explained. "Their clothes were a little off, all wearing sunglasses early in the morning - that kind of thing. But it wasn't just the morning; after the bombs started going off and I was trying to get out of the city to get my family, I would come across packs of them fighting, running through the streets with AKs and setting up choke-points, coordinating taking out cars on either end of a busy block and then walking up the line of cars in between and spraying on full auto, killing every helpless man, woman and child trapped inside."

"Jesus."

"Yeah, it was a little ruthless. I got a few of 'em on my way back. I take the train in to work and I guess one of the first things they bombed were the public transit routes out of the city. The reports were saying the train and bus stations were rocked with explosions at the same time."

"All Arabs?"

"I'm not sure, man, I just know what I saw. If I had to put a name on them...I don't know... I'm pretty sure they were Persians and Lebanese. Is it possible that Quds and Hezbollah are working together?"

"Wouldn't be the first time, Brother," Josh replied.

"Anyway," Adam continued, "I got a few of them. I grabbed one of the cars they shot up. Didn't have any weapons, but luckily enough they were just several blocks away when I started driving. Two of them had their back to me, shooting up cars, when I turned them into speed bumps. I took their AKs and ammo, got in the car and moved back to the house."

"Right," chimed in Josh. "So we know we're dealing with Arabs; Quds would make a lot of sense as we know Iran has been looking for a way to hit us for a long time. Anybody want to cover our little bump on the way back?"

"Yeah," laughed Buckeye. "That was a new one."

His comment was met with the laugh of an inside joke by the others who had been with them.

"We were well over halfway back with Adam and family in tow. Right about...here," Buckeye said as he pointed to a spot on the map that seemed to be where Fort Campbell was located. "We saw something come up on the Blue Force Tracker. I was in the lead truck when the call came that we were coming up on friendlies, a couple of HUMVEEs. They were still a few miles out, headed toward us at a pretty fast speed when all of a sudden they stopped, and we began to watch helos without any markings come into the picture."

"Bad guys?" J-Lo asked.

"You got that right," Buckeye replied. "Turns out they were a group of Infantry from the 101st who had time to organize and mobilize, but the enemy located where they were and set up a nasty ambush for them along the highway."

"Wait a minute," I said, scratching my head and trying to put the pieces together. "When and how the hell would Iran get helos here?"

"That's the thing," answered Josh. "They weren't Iranian helos. They were Russian."

"Great, just great. Sorry I asked."

"It gets better," Josh said with a smirk. "Keep listening."

"Yeah," continued Buckeye. "So the ambush had been going for about fifteen minutes before we even got there, and let's just say they made short work of our boys. Lucky for us, they didn't keep their heads on a swivel or expect anyone else to come out to play because they weren't ready for us."

He glanced around the room, seeming to search for some confirmation from the other guys before continuing to give his account of the action.

"As soon as the helos stopped moving, we realized they were searching the area and bodies for any intelligence they could find and coming down on the objective. They were sitting ducks, man. The helo was on the ground with rotors off when the ambushers came down from their positions, and it was open season. We thought about going in there quietly, but Tattoo sent the Raven out ahead of us for a closer look, and Josh made the call to get 'em while their pants were down."

Tattoo added his piece next.

"I could see they weren't even paying attention to anything. No situational awareness whatsoever. They sat on the objective, smoking, joking, and pulling our guys out of the HUMVEEs to search their pockets," he said.

"It was like shooting fish in a barrel," continued Buckeye. We rolled in with the .50cal first, took out the helo and all but two of the soldiers. Jason got them in just a few shots as soon as he got out of his truck."

"Good job, guys," said Matty, smiling.

"Yeah, but not so fast, Bro. They caught us with our pants down too," laughed Josh.

Buckeye continued, "So we got caught in the same exact situation, but thankfully, we had a good luck charm named Tattoo."

"It wasn't anything special," said Tattoo. "Josh tracked the helo coming in and gave me a heads up, so I had a few seconds to get the AT4 ready, and it was just a matter of aiming once it flew over the mountain."

"Wait a minute! You took down a freaking helicopter with an AT4?" I asked incredulously.

"Damn right he did! Give me some of that," Josh smiled as he went for a fist bump with Tattoo.

The room was silent for a moment as we stared at Tattoo and picked our jaws up off the floor. We'd all seen it in movies, but the reality of bringing down a helo with an AT4, RPG or any shoulder-fired missile that wasn't a Stinger with heat-seeking capabilities was the proverbial shooting the nuts off a mosquito - except this mosquito was equipped with radar, chaff, and every bit of technology one could imagine.

"So how was the rest of the ride?" asked J-Lo.

"Pretty nice, actually. I never realized how beautiful that part of the country is this time of year," Josh remarked.

CHAPTER 5

PICKING A FIGHT

With only a few hours to work before the final convoy came in, Jason, Adam and I chose to spend that time in the clinic going over our medical items. Our top priority was to ensure everything be cataloged with location and expiration date, and that each of us knew how to use every piece of equipment and medication.

That's the very nature of emergency medicine; by its definition, it is needed in a state of emergency and when one is under quite a bit of stress and you don't know everything like the back of your hand, you're probably going to screw up.

Matty poked his head in to announce eagles coming in, and the team headed directly upstairs. It had been a long time since most of us last saw Bulldog, and we were eager to greet him.

Our former commander, Bulldog was assigned to a different group when his time on 022 came to an end. Like all Special Forces officers, he transitioned to staff after finishing his team time and never let us forget how much he favored the field over his new desk.

Since not all of the team were on active duty anymore, the question arose during our planning of whether or not we would each be able to actually make it to the compound if our protocols were ever set into motion.

Due to The Posse Comitatus Act, active duty military aren't allowed to operate within our nations borders unless Congress declared Martial Law, leaving the nation's defense to the National Guard.

Knowing one of the first steps in an invasion would be taking down our communications grid, we understood that would leave the country defenseless.

Without the ability to call National Guard troops in, they wouldn't be able to organize in time to fend off an attack, and the people would be on their own.

In the end, it was Bulldog who made it painstakingly clear that - active duty or not - fighting was our outright duty if the time came - no matter what the cost or consequences.

Congress made it painfully obvious their decisions weren't in the best interest of the American people and in Bulldog's mind, that left us no other option.

There wasn't a doubt in any of our minds that none of the spineless politicians would risk their neck in an emergency meeting to declare Martial Law, but would most likely be running for the hills at the first sign of trouble.

As Bulldog pointed out during our planning, it was our job description and duty as Green Berets to do what we do best: guerrilla warfare.

As soon as we had all gathered around in the conference room, he laid out exactly how we were going to do just that.

An athletic man in his late thirties, Bulldog got his name not only because he reminded us of The Duke in both leadership qualities and personality, but also because, well, he slightly resembled a very good-looking bulldog.

It was obvious he knew exactly what he was going to say, and the instant he slapped the telescopic pointer on the map, he owned every one of our attention.

"Here we are," he said, pointing to the green dot representing our compound. "We're fighting a multitude of enemies on this one, boys, and they were very cunning as to how they went about their infil."

"Multiple enemies?" I asked.

"Right now our intelligence shows we're dealing with the Iranian Special Forces, or Quds, and Hezbollah, who are being found scattered across the East Coast. Here in the middle of the country we are encountering mainly Russians, and reports from the West Coast indicate Russians are leading the assault there as well."

He paused, scanning the room to ensure we followed before continuing.

"Their execution was brilliant, exactly as we would have done trying to take on a superior force with weak borders. Somehow they infiltrated, set off explosions in major population centers all across the country, caused chaos, took down the power grid and, while our attention was diverted, they brought in the heavy troops and equipment."

"Any word if we're fighting back?" inquired Chris.

"I only had time to get a few initial reports, and they aren't good," answered Bulldog.

"They took down the power and communication grids before the National Guard had a chance to recall their troops, meaning the phone systems are out and there's no real way to get a hold of them. The classified NIPR network was still up when I left, but I'm not sure how long that will last."

He scanned the room for questions and, not finding any, continued.

"Word came down from USASOC [United States Special Operations Command] for everyone in Special Forces to grab as much gear, weapons and ammo as we could and do as much damage to the enemy as possible. The conventional units may try to launch some sort of front, but it's our job to create chaos within their ranks and keep them on their heels long enough for them to put something together."

"Then enough with the talk and let's get to work," Griz exclaimed from the corner.

"Well said," replied Bulldog.

"But you know how we do it. We have just over a dozen soldiers, they have tens of thousands. Let's put a plan together before we run in head first."

Josh stepped in, saying, "We know they need to take the major cities before focusing on the more rural areas and suburbs, so let's start with Denver."

"What do you guys think?" asked Bulldog, looking around the room for the slightest bit of worry or hesitation. "You want to jump in with both feet and go to Denver, no confidence targets on the periphery first?"

"Screw a confidence hit," Ray. "We've been doing this long enough. I think Rob's been out of the game the longest, but I know he can still shoot. I say we're ready!"

"Well alright then," smiled Bulldog, just as glad as any of us that we were heading directly into the fire.

"We leave in six hours for our first mission. We need to figure out who's going to be our recon, main force, and of course, who's staying back here. Josh and I will break everyone up into their assignments; you guys get some food, rest, and spend time with your families. Meet back here in one hour."

As the team began to exit the room, I made a beeline for the group who arrived on the last convoy.

"Big Tone, how the hell are you doing, Brother?" I asked Tony, one of my big brothers in Special Forces who, along with Chris and Josh, had basically been one of my father figures on my first ODA and shown me the ropes.

Tony met my bear hug with equal force, and the grin on his muscular jaw was big enough for me to feel during the embrace before I stepped back to get a good look at him. He had been reassigned to a different group entirely after his time on 022 was up, and I hadn't seen him in years.

Thankfully, he kept in contact with Chris and Ray. I felt better and safer with him around. Between he, Josh, Chris and Bulldog, our team contained more combat experience than anyone could ask for, and I was feeling pretty good about our situation.

"Chad! Griz! What's up, Brothers?" I asked, putting both hands up in front of me for fist bumps, which were promptly met with their knuckles and subsequent bear hugs.

Griz and I spent time together on 022, working in the misery of the B-team in Afghanistan, and had always gotten along like blood brothers.

He personified a mountain man through and through, loving nothing more than hunting, fishing, and living off the land, and was about as tough as a grizzly bear in the midst of spring, hence his name. He was a perennial bachelor, and his striking Nordic features and good looks meant he never found himself hard up for a date.

Chad and I also met during my time on 022 while stationed in Germany together, but we became closest while deployed to Iraq together on my last trip with the Army.

He could be downright terrifying at first glance if you didn't know him, given that he stood around 6'5, weighed in at 240 pounds with arms the size of tree trunks.

Coupled with python-like veins bulging out of his bronze skin, you knew if you crossed him he could most likely pull your arms clean-off like a kid with the wings of a mosquito.

With chiseled facial features and eyes that were usually covered by a pair of dark Oakley sunglasses, he always seemed to size you up, looking right through even the smallest amount of bullshit you may be feeding him.

Chad, however, was quite the opposite. He was one of the nicest, funniest and kindest people I ever met, and he never failed to crack me up when I would visit him and Laurie.

Eastern European by birth, she was an extremely kind, earth-conscious and funny redhead. When standing next to her hulk of a husband, together they resembled the image of King Kong carrying his loving bride to the top of the empire state building.

As Chad was pulling his massive arms from around my neck, there was a tap on my shoulder, and when I turned around, I was met by the enormous and shining grin of my Brother, Corey.

About my size, Corey was another brunette whose strikingly boyish good looks always made me think he should have been a GI Joe action figure. He had been my first senior medic on 022, and taught me the ins and outs of what it meant to be a good one.

He was with me on my first trip to Africa for a medical relief mission. Along with my experiences on that trip, he played a large role in my passion for medicine and drive to become a doctor.

Some medics truly hated that job, and some tolerated it. But there are those like Corey, Adam and I who found their true calling as 18Ds and knew immediately that we were right where we belonged.

Jason had been a Marine Infantryman before crossing over to Special Forces and becoming an 18 Delta. Although he was one of the best medics around, I knew deep down he loved shooting bad guys in the face much more than patching people up.

He stood tall and lean and had the chiseled features of a professional baseball player and the boy-next-door attributes that made you trust him instantly. Never one to sugarcoat the truth, his honesty and bluntness were characteristics I always cherished.

With an immanent mission in our hands, we immediately went on autopilot. One of the major differences between Special Forces guys and the rest of the military is that we have our implied tasks, so we each knew what needed to be done without instruction in order to get ready and roll out the gate on our first mission.

As such, us medics naturally drifted to the medical room to begin packing our bags, putting our gear and equipment on the trucks, and ensuring each of us knew where every bit of it was located on the vehicles.

This was especially useful when we needed it to work on ourselves, as it's a long-standing truth in Special Forces that, as per Murphy's Law, the medic is always the first guy hit.

As we would take new bags to strap on the sides and trunk of our trucks, we found the Bravos (weapons guys) hard at work making sure the guns were lubed up and ready to rock, and just as we with the medical equipment, they spent their time finding every square inch of real estate possible to load with ammo and/or weapons.

I could hear the Echos (communications guys) working on the radios from the other side of the garage, testing to make sure they worked in every possible configuration.

Commo was the most confusing job to guys in Special Forces. We medics could teach anyone to patch a bullet hole, the Bravos could teach anyone to shoot a gun, and the Charlies could teach anyone to build a bomb and blow a door of its hinges, but the radios were nothing more than boxes full of magic elves who made the words come out as far as any of us were concerned and thankfully, between Matty, Chad and Griz, we had the best commo guys any of us had ever met.

As I was walking away from the garage and pondering how lucky we were to have the best and the brightest found across all jobs for an ODA, I heard Matty and Chad testing two of the radios, making the classic Beavis and Butthead impressions.

"Uhhhh...syphilis....uh....huhuhuhuh...that's what she said."

Only seasoned Green Berets could find humor in a situation like that.

The compound was built with each respective group having their own areas, so once we were done with the medical equipment and preparation, I made my way over to the Charlie area.

That was where the engineers were working on every type of explosive we would require for the mission, and I was curious to see what they were getting into.

We intentionally made the decision to put the Charlie area as far away as possible, unconnected from the rest of the underground compound because, well, if one of those guys made even the slightest mistake with the thousands of pounds of C4, blasting caps, dynamite and other black-side explosives we made off with over the years, we ran the risk of losing the entire compound in one sitting.

During my time in the Army and medical school, I worked with many people in the highest of high-stress professions, and it was always a great testament of character to see how people performed under such stress. I was not disappointed when I walked into the Charlie area.

Walking down the dust-covered stairs to enter the Charlie lair, I was met with the echoes of laughter, steadily growing louder as I descended. Upon passing through the thick metal shipping container doors, my first sight was of Ray.

He stood on a table in the middle of the room, stick of dynamite in his crotch, dancing in a circle like a cowboy riding a horse as the guys sat at the table laughing like hyenas.
Classic.

Everyone else at the table around him were working on shape charges to blow doors off their hinges, claymores to take out enemy soldiers in ambushes, and huge anti-tank charges to blow anything into oblivion.

I couldn't help but laugh myself. Most people would be terrified working around this level of explosives, giving themselves a heart attack if they heard a mouse fart.

But our guys had enough brushes with real life-or-death situations and the nerves of steel to still be able to have fun and crack jokes while sitting on and around enough high explosives to blow up several small cities.

Ray turned to me, smiling with dynamite still in hand and called out, "Hey, Rob, did ya see what Bulldog brought us?"

Before I could respond, several fist-sized balls were sent flying through the air toward my face via Tony, and I realized what they were the moment they landed in my hands.

"He made off with a few dozen cases of frag grenades," Ray said. "He remembered they were the only thing we've been missing and he came through like a boss."

Tossing the frags back in forth between my hands, I was pleasantly surprised. Grenades could really turn the tide in a fight and were the one thing we couldn't adequately make.

We acquired more ammo than we could ever use over the past several years, built our own reloading room to fashion homemade bullets, had plenty of bombs and materials to produce them, but there remained something about the size and consistency of a frag that the guys had never been able to get quite right.

"You mind taking those to the team room and handing them out?" Chris asked.

"Sure thing," I said, still tossing the handfuls of death back and forth between my hands, glad the pieces of our puzzle were coming together so well.

Bulldog and Josh were the only ones in the team room when I arrived, still busy setting up the logistics for our first mission and breaking us down into different elements to conduct our attack.

While a conventional unit would have a relatively large amount of people and logistical support to send after a target, a Special Forces team rarely did.

That everyone was cross-trained and could do any job on the team in a pinch made it a bit easier, but as each of us had a different repertoire of skills and experiences, it was extremely important to ensure the right guy be assigned to the right job.

"We've still got about thirty minutes before we regroup to start planning," Josh told me. "Go hang out with the kids."

"Roger that," I replied, and ducked out of the room before they had time to change their minds.

I found Sarah, Ray's wife, reading the kids a book before their nap when I got down to the room, so I quietly snuck into bed beside them, cradling my daughter in my arms.

My son became immediately jealous and crawled closer so I could encircle both of them in my embrace, which in turn made Avery jealous and made her crawl on my chest to try to be the closest to daddy.

Their mother and I dated while I was in Special Forces, but for all intents and purposes, I had been single during my combat deployments. We married within weeks of my leaving the Army as she swore she would never marry a Green Beret, and within a week of the wedding, we were pregnant with Robert.

A large part of my outlook on life and the world naturally changed once I had my kids, and as I sat in bed with everything that I truly loved in my arms, I couldn't fathom the amount of sadness that must have been in the other guys' hearts with wives and kids at home while we were away, jumping out of airplanes and helicopters and getting into firefights with terrorists.

But even they had the luxury of separation. Though it must have been tough to talk to their families on Skype and then walk straight to the trucks to go on a mission, at least once the phone was hung up, they could go back into soldier mode, with nothing but the mission at hand to focus on.

Laying with my family in my arms, knowing shortly I'd have to leave them there and go back to war was a daunting task, and I wasn't sure I was going to be able to do it.

Thankfully, J-Lo made it easy for me. The moment the full weight of Avery's head fell into my forearm and her breathing turned to the slow rhythm of sleep, I saw movement in the doorway as a pair of boots stopped their steps at the front of our room.

"Hey, Rob," J-Lo whispered.

"What's up, Bro?" I asked, sitting up so I could see his outline in the doorway.

"Josh and Bulldog are ready for us. They want everyone in the team room in five."

I nodded and gave him a thumbs-up. I kissed Avery and Robert on their foreheads and swung my legs over to put my feet on the ground. My morning ritual had always been to meditate for a few minutes before getting up and out of bed, but I knew I didn't have that kind of time.

I found the guys standing around the large table in the middle of the team room, every inch of which was covered with military maps of the area. Our names were broken down into groups on the whiteboard at the front of the room, designating who would be operating in which element.

We would be broken down into command and control, a recon/sniper element, and an attack force. The recon team would be sent out first on motorcycles with the Ravens (small, hand held drones) so they could cover as much ground as quickly as possible. It wasn't the safest option, but speed seemed to be our best option for safety, so that was what we were going with.

Our mission was to conduct unconventional warfare, the hallmark of Special Forces, and the best time to do so is before the enemy has time to get their feet on the ground and settle in.

One of the problems this created for a smaller force like ours was a lack of resources for reconnaissance, whereas a traditional unit or military would have access to planes, satellites and the like to choose their targets and plan.

Although we didn't have a sophisticated recon network in place, there was one surefire location we knew the enemy would be establishing a base as soon as possible.

There are a few basic rules in warfare - no matter the doctrine, country or training involved.

At the top of the list is the need to secure large landing areas to begin bringing in conventional forces and equipment as quickly as possible so you can maintain any momentum gained in the initial assault.

This is why the Allied Forces lost so many brave men on Normandy Beach in 1944, why our current Rangers spend so much of their time building an entire doctrine based on airfield seizure, and why we knew that if the enemy were anywhere, they'd be at Denver International Airport (DIA).

We had enough medics between us to put one with each team, and as I had been out of action for a few years, my place was with the command & control element. This meant I'd still be on the objective, but following the main assault force, helping Josh and

Bulldog coordinate rather than kicking down doors and leading the fight.

Corey was a certified sniper, so he'd be heading out with the recon element, while Jason would be leading the assault with the guys.

One of us had to stay back to make sure someone was present in case the families got sick or hurt, and more importantly, so we didn't lose all of our medics in one sitting if this operation went horribly wrong. As the one who was the last to arrive among us and most in need of some downtime, Adam was given that responsibility.

Our planning brief lasted less than an hour during which we were given our assignments, communications plan, signals to attack, retreat or regroup, as well as our routes.

We understood DIA would be a hub of activity, acting as a central base that would be sending its forces out using a wheel-and-spoke methodology, so we couldn't take any main roads.

Fortunately, Colorado was lousy with side streets and farm roads due to the large population of ranches, so it wasn't a problem to find primary and secondary routes in.

After Josh and Bulldog finished briefing us on the mission plan, we divvied up equipment, made sure our radios and night vision goggles worked, packed every bit of ammo and explosives possible into our rucksacks and walked outside with the recon element to say goodbye.

Recon was the most dangerous part of a mission like this, but also the most necessary. It was our normal procedure to place an element with eyes on the target for at least forty-eight hours before we executed a mission, but with the need to hit the enemy before they could organize, time wasn't a luxury we had on our side.

It was an absolute necessity to get them in for as long in advance of the hit as possible because despite having all of our maps and plans, we had no real-time knowledge of their forces, the amount of men they had, the kind of weapons they were armed with and how much equipment they had on the ground already. We didn't even know which countries they were from!

The most dangerous part of any recon mission - especially this one - was that they had no immediate backup. At least a mission with the whole team could carry enough firepower to buy some time and find our way out of trouble, but if a one or two-man element gets himself seen, it's game over.

As we had been a Special Reconnaissance team, our Charlies procured the best telescopes, radios, cameras, and recon equipment money could buy, outfitting this mission quite well.

But no matter how advanced our gear, they needed to be especially careful because the airport, located in central Colorado, was flat, covered a lot of distance and was wide open.

We needed to inflict a lot of damage as quickly as possible and get out before the enemy had time to regroup, so we decided on two main targets: the main terminal (where we guessed they would most logically be setting up their headquarters) and the air traffic control tower. If they couldn't land any planes, the airport was no good to them.

Although there weren't any mountains close enough to hide our recon elements and only a few scattered main roads to move our assault through, we did find something that would work in our favor: rivers along the northeast, northwest, and southwest boundaries of the airport.

The northeast and northwest rivers could take a small element close enough to two of the runways to place a few of our large anti-tank mines daisy-chained together in order to render them inoperable for landing of more troops and equipment. Meanwhile, the southwest river ended at the third runway.

The decision was made that if the recon elements couldn't get into the riverbeds and out of sight, we'd call off the entire mission, they'd come home and we'd devise another plan.

If they couldn't safely get onto the runways and plant their charges, they'd give us an assessment of whether the assault force could get in to do any damage or if it would be a suicide mission.

As a last resort, our route would be taking us through an urban environment with enough buildings to conceal our movement, so if we couldn't successfully engage the airport terminals, we could still bomb the last runway en route and accomplish something for the night.

But if there were a way to get our assault force close enough to attack the terminals and for the recon element to get those charges on the runway, it would be our first chance to inflict some serious damage.

The greatest factor we were counting on was still time. DIA covered a lot of ground, and to secure that much terrain and put fences, guard outposts and security up would take more than a few days.

Even if the enemy had already began landing planes with conventional troops, they'd still be tired, confused and unorganized, so striking while the iron was hot would be our best security, even if we were hitting the target that was likely to have the largest force.

The entire team was present to see the recon element off. With explosives packed into the storage boxes on their motorcycles and backpacks full of ammo, they rode off several hours before any of us, splitting up to take three different routes as soon as they hit the first main road outside of our compound.

The moment they were out of sight and the gates were closed, we got back to work.

Depending on what intelligence the recon element sent back to us, there were several options for the night's mission.

It was either driving right onto the objective in our trucks with the big guns and plenty of ammo, or having to ditch the vehicles and walk onto the objective through the rivers and under concealment as the recon element had. The third option, which would be utilized in a worst-case scenario, was being a rescue mission to go get our guys out of trouble.

We had to be prepared for anything, ready to change the entire mission on a moments notice, so we packed accordingly.

The recon element had only been gone for an hour by the time we set out with the main assault force.

They would travel a lot faster than us on their motorcycles and would utilize terrain that we wouldn't be able to cover in the trucks, so we figured they'd have plenty of time on the ground to give us the go/no-go criteria for the mission before we were close.

By the time we rolled out of the gate, I felt like I had never left the team, instantly becoming more comfortable back in my body armor, shooting gloves, boots and uniform than I had ever been in scrubs and a white lab coat.

The solid grip of my M4 handle in one hand and M203 grenade launcher in the other gave me a strange sense of balance and purpose, and I was eager to get on the battlefield.

The ride into a mission can be the longest time of your life as you incessantly cover the plans in your head, go over things you're supposed to do and things that can go wrong, all the while looking out for an enemy who may or may not know you're coming.

It was almost two hours of staring out of my window at the night vision, green-illuminated Colorado landscape before Matty's voice shattered the silence in my peltors.

"Trojan four, this is Echo two. We're set."

"Roger, Echo two," Bulldog replied. "What's the SITREP [Situation Report]?"

"It's a go. We got in without any trouble and only saw four unarmored vehicles doing roving security. The only perimeter is the airport fencing and we can get through with our wire cutters. There's a lot of activity in the main terminal, but it's mostly inside. All I see are logistical operations with minimal security. You're cleared hot for now."

"Roger. Let us know if the situation changes. We should be on target in twenty mics."

Bulldog turned around to speak to the rest of the truck.

"Everyone hear that?" he asked. "We're cleared hot. Remember what we went over in the brief. We're not here to try to take on the force; just to cause a distraction for the guys to get those charges on the runway and get the hell out. First target of opportunity we find to inflict a little damage and make some noise, we'll hit and get out!"

Everyone in the truck nodded in agreement while Griz stuck his hand down from the gun turret to give a thumbs up. The tension escalated with every passing second and by the looks of the terrain speeding past my window, I knew we were getting close.

When we turned onto the farm road that would take us almost all the way to the objective, I tightened the grip on my rifle and readied myself.

As Matty indicated, we easily made it all the way to the perimeter without being spotted. Some dismounted to cover the Charlies, cutting a hole in the fence big enough for our vehicles with the Broco torches we utilized on countless fences surrounding the compounds of high-level terrorists in Iraq.

I used the time to take a quick view of the objective through the sight on my rifle and was pleased to see what had been hoped for in our best-case-scenario plan. The airport was filled with soldiers unloading trucks and containers, carrying supplies into hangars and the main terminal with hardly any security.

The lights were on in the terminal and soldiers walked around in front of the unprotected windows, doing exactly what we had hoped: unsuspecting any kind of attack so soon in the game and immediately spreading themselves too thin, leaving their headquarters wide open.

Ray finished making HUMVEE-sized holes in the perimeter fence and as he walked back towards the trucks, we climbed back in and took up our positions.

In a conventional war, we would have used artillery, mortars, air assets and support forces to lay down suppressive fire long before we got to the objective. But we were all we had on this mission, and we hoped it would be enough.

Taking his seat in our truck after putting the Broco torch and equipment away, Ray and I looked to Bulldog for approval. A slight nod from him told me all I needed to know, and I slammed my boot down on the accelerator to carry us back onto the battlefield.

As our trucks moved through the new holes cut out of the fence, I noticed movement ahead of us that took me a moment to comprehend. Like a scene out of a military cartoon, the ground before us began to tremble and open up in dozens of locations around the airfield.

Suddenly, the soil opened in hatches across the terrain, giving way to soldiers being lifted to ground level on hydraulic systems, each one in full battle uniform and heavily armed.

I was dumbstruck with awe, a part of me wondering if this was a dream, when Bulldog, who still had his faculties about him, called out to the team over the radio.

"What the hell is that?" he yelled into his mic, astonished.

"They look like Americans, sir!" Tattoo exclaimed, coming over the net from his spot to our northeast.

"That doesn't mean they are. I've never heard of any military elements here," Bulldog responded.

As if to answer his question, the squad-sized groups of soldiers began firing and running towards the enemy the instant they were above ground, and were moving with amazing speed.

We watched them drop to the ground and set up mortars and heavy machine guns, and as they shot shoulder-fired rockets at the enemy helicopters trying to take off, we knew they were on our team.

"Get those charges on the airfield! Assault element, let's focus on that main terminal," commanded Bulldog over the radio.

While our newfound allies were maneuvering towards the enemy containers, vehicles and enemy on the ground, we pointed our trucks in the direction of the terminal and sped towards them as fast as we could.

I was glad we had friends on the objective; even if the airport wasn't heavily fortified yet, the distance we were covering to reach the terminal was a lot more than it seemed on the map.

When we were within range to do some damage on the terminal with our big guns, the drivers stopped the trucks and prepared to attack.

With the Barrett .50 cal and .300 Winmag sniper rifles out from the trunks, and our machine guns erupting with fire, we set in on the ground with our rifles and proceeded to turn the terminal into a shooting gallery.

Through the scope of my rifle, it was clear to see we had caught the enemy completely off-guard. The first rule in a war zone is to never get lazy or complacent, and this was a textbook example of just how disastrous the consequences were for the side who took their eyes off the ball.

The windows in the terminal hadn't been reinforced yet, and with a team highly trained in long distance and high-angle targeting, we were shooting fish in a barrel.

In between acquiring and neutralizing targets, I caught myself glancing over at the strangers fighting on our side, my mind trying to make sense of who or what they were.

The enemy soldiers inside the terminal seemed to be logistical personnel with little combat training, as even after dozens of their colleagues were on the ground dying from our precisely-aimed rounds through the windows, they would continue running right in front of the shattered glass, only to add numbers to our final kill count.

As I rolled over on my side to change the magazine of my rifle, I paused and watched for a moment as the strangers fighting on our side continued to push forward.

They reached the opposite end of the terminal from where we were firing, and without so much as a pause, they began running through the exterior doors and using ladders to scale the wall and climb in through shattered windows.

I couldn't help but think that with such flawless execution and no need for direction, they must have rehearsed these actions a thousand times.

Matty was the first to report his charges set on the northwest runway, with Tattoo and Chris not far behind. Bulldog paused to study the runways, moved to depress his push-to-talk, but paused when he noticed a faint light in the night sky.

Through a pause in the cacophony of gunfire and battle, I heard what grabbed his attention: several enemy cargo planes making their descent.

Bulldog turned to Josh and asked, "Think we can keep this up for another few minutes?"

In response, Josh began to pick up the AT4s he had staged in preparation and began handing them out.

"I think we've got that covered, sir," he said, grinning.

"Echo two, Bravo two, Charlie one, wait. Don't blow those charges until the cargo plane is landing; don't do it too early or they'll wave off. Try to get a 2-for-1 with this charge."

"That's my runway," replied Matty. "I got this."

We took turns exchanging sniper rifles for AT4s as Bulldog patiently watched the cargo planes approach.

As the first one began its final descent onto the runway, he spoke into his microphone to the recon element, hiding in wait with fingers on the initiators.

"Steady, boys," he spoke softly.

Its nose came up as the landing gear came down.

"Just a few more seconds."

The plane dropped speed and began descending rapidly.

"Patience guys, patience. On my mark; I have control, I have control, I have control," he said, not wanting to miss the perfect opportunity to deal a huge blow to the enemy's morale.

The back wheels came down and Bulldog's body tensed. The nose touched down next, and as soon as the brakes engaged he gave the command.

"Blow 'em to hell, boys."

Not a second after the command was given, a dull thud shook the ground beneath us as all three runways lit up the sky, enveloping the enemy planes in enormous balls of fire.

"Recon element, get out of there!" shouted Bulldog. "Assault, as soon as they call in they're on the bikes, we're pulling back!"

Pointing to a row of empty military vehicles a few hundred meters away, Bulldog shouted into his mic.

"Rob! Buckeye! Get over there and commandeer a couple of those vehicles, preferably the ones with guns!"

I looked across the firing line at Buckeye, gave him a wink and started running.

"Race you there!" I yelled, smiling back at him. "Cover me while I move."

The flurry of .50 cal rounds erupted into the now empty window frames of the main terminal as we ran, and Tattoo called in as I was reaching the first vehicle in line - an American Bradley fighting vehicle, complete with big guns up top. I wasn't exactly sure what it was doing there but for the time being I wasn't asking either.

As I watched Buckeye jump into the driver's seat of a Soviet-style deuce and a half two ton truck full of crates in the back and crank the engine, I engaged the ignition on the Bradley and got ready to move.

"Bravo two, exfil!" I heard Tattoo yell into his mic as he raced away from the objective.

"Lead truck, get in and let's get ready!" shouted Josh.

As I floored the accelerator and starting driving towards our holes in the fence, Chris called
in his exit.

"Charlie one, exfil."

"Let's get a move on! I don't want to be here when the reinforcements show up," yelled Bulldog.

"Echo two, exfil." Matty called in as I neared the fence line.

"Everybody in the trucks, let's get the hell out of here!" yelled Josh.

As I drove through the fence, not quite fitting into the holes and taking part of it along with me, I could see the last of the ground troops maneuvering towards the terminal.

Who the hell are those guys? I wondered.

In the end, it didn't matter; we just scored a huge first victory over the enemy and we owed a big part of it to them - whoever they were.

CHAPTER 6

STARTING OVER

Driving back to our base through the desolate and
apocalyptic streets of downtown Denver, I caught the glimpse of an
ever-familiar symbol out of the corner of my eye.

"Stop Stop Stop Stop!" I yelled into my mic.

As the lead truck slammed on its brakes, I started to apply my
own, watching the entire convoy screech to a halt as Bulldog
screamed over the net through my Peltors.

"What is it? IED? Ambush? Distance and direction!" he bellowed
into his radio.

"We have to go back!" I shouted into my mic.

"What the hell do you mean we have to go back?" he screamed.
"We just left a crater in a major center of their operations! That
place is gonna be crawling with heavy weapons any minute now -
there's no going back!"

"Not to the objective, sir. A block back. We have to go back
there."

"What the hell are you talking about, Rob?"

I didn't know how to explain it; if we were in the business of
saving our country we needed to go back to what I had seen,
although I knew the guys wouldn't understand.

"Follow me," I yelled into my mic. I made a u-turn and began to
make my way through a few abandoned and burned out cars to head

back. Looking into the side mirrors I saw the rest of our convoy following suit, so I charged ahead.

Being the only Freemason on the team, I knew the other guys wouldn't get it, having been inundated with the same conspiracy theories as the rest of the population to think Masons were evil and up to no good.

But I knew better, having been one myself for quite some time. And even if I were wrong about my hunch, it was my duty to make sure.

I pulled the Bradley to a screeching halt at the front of the building I had seen, sitting atop a staircase leading up to the symbol that represented everything I stood for.

The rest of the convoy stopped as I sprinted up the steps, approached the door and did what I had so many times before under very different circumstances.

Knock, Knock, Knock. The plastic shell covering the gloves over my knuckles met the thick oak door three times, letting anyone inside know I was not only a friendly, but also a Brother.

"What the hell, Rob?" Josh asked as he exited his truck and walked to the bottom of the stairs to yell at me.

"There's nobody here. Anyone left in this town is either in a concentration camp, dead or headed for the hills. We don't have time to sit here and screw around!"

"Just give me a second, Josh" I replied, waving him off.

"We don't have a second!" he said. "There are Russian helicopters and enemy soldiers from

God knows how many different countries looking to find and kill us right now, we need to get the hell out of here."

"I got it!" I shot back to him. "But there are civilians here and we need to get them out."

"What the hell makes you think there are civilians here, Rob? We don't have time for your BS. Get your butt in the truck and let's get on the road!"

I glanced at my watch. I had only been waiting a minute, but if nobody answered the door yet, well, maybe I was wrong. I turned and had started down the stairs when I heard a voice from the other side of the door ask me with an ever-familiar question.

"From whence came you?" questioned the ancient voice on the other end.

My subconscious recognized the question before it even registered, and without thinking I turned around and gave the answer I had given many times before to greet my masonic Brothers, my brethren.

"From the Lodge of Saint James in Israel," I heard myself reply, and as with every time, a warm sense of familiarity and ease washed over my mind and body.

Within seconds, the oak door creaked open, revealing an old man with a long, grey beard on the other side of the door, standing proudly with a big smile on his face.

"I knew you were coming, Brother!" he exclaimed. "How many can you take?"

I shot a glance back to Josh whose astonished expression said all that needed to be said.

"How many do you have?" I asked the old man.

"We've been evacuating schools and trying to find the children's families to hide them here, so we have an awful lot. But we're running out of food and water to sustain them all. The Brothers of the Lodge will stay, but we'd appreciate you taking their families and the others if you can."

"We'll make room, Brother," I answered. "Get them ready. As many as we can fit are welcome with us, but we need to move quickly."

"Drive your vehicles around back," he directed. "Our parking lot is covered so the helicopters won't see you. I'll rouse the civilians and start sending them out."

"Is the Lodge room open?" I asked.

He answered me by saying, "You know that you cannot bring weapons of war into a Lodge room, but it is always open for a Brother."

The old man turned and began to walk back into the large entry room, gently limping against his cane, and started barking orders to other men located in the hallway.

I turned to Josh, still standing behind me, dumbfounded.

"I've got something I have to do. Can you drive the Bradley around back? I'll start helping load the civilians in a few minutes."

"Yeah, man," Josh replied. "How did you...?" he began to ask.

"No time to explain now, but I promise I will when the time is right."

As Josh turned to head back down the stairs, I turned back to the hallway, closed the heavy door and safely secured the locks. I had never stepped foot in this Lodge before, but I knew precisely where I was going.

A few dozen steps down a hallway, through the dining room and down another hallway, I came to a room behind two large double doors, amidst walls adorned with pictures of presidents, generals and founders of our great nation.

Walking past the couches and to another set of thick, wooden double doors, I looked to my right and saw a finely decorated sword leaning against the wall.

Taking a deep breath and smelling an ever-familiar scent, I took off my rifle, helmet, and body armor and laid them down next to the sword.

Devoid of my metal and weapons, I centered myself and swung open the doors to a cavernous, well-decorated room, the likes of which I had spent many an evening in.

I took my thirty-three steps Eastward into the room and knelt before the altar, upon which lay the Bible. Opening it to the book of Psalms, I took a deep breath and read aloud.

"The Lord is my shepherd; I shall not want. He maketh me to lie down in green pastures: he leadeth me beside the still waters. He restoreth my soul: he leadeth me in the paths of righteousness for his name's sake.

Yea, though I walk through the valley of the shadow of death, I will fear no evil: for thou art with me; thy rod and thy staff they comfort me.

Thou preparest a table before me in the presence of mine enemies: thou anointest my head with oil; my cup runneth over. Surely goodness and mercy shall follow me all the days of my life: and I will dwell in the house of the Lord forever."

I closed the heavy, ancient book softly, stood and made the sign of the cross, bowed my head, and paused to salute the American flag standing proudly in the corner. I felt a single warm tear leave my eye and begin its journey down my scruffy face.

These three things had done more to help mend a shattered soul after my years in war. The solace I found in the Bible, the Lodge and the Flag strengthened me and gave me that which I needed in my heart to keep me going, to do the terrible things which I knew lay ahead to protect my family, my country, and my Brothers.

As I turned to leave the room, I saw the old man, standing just inside the doors, watching me.

A small nod told me he would be with me in soul and spirit, but it was time to get back to business.

He waited silently as I donned my weapons and armor and led me to the back door and our waiting vehicles. The last of the children were being loaded into our trucks. Bulldog caught my eye and spoke into his mic.

"Alright, we've got a lot more reasons now to be careful and tread this one quietly. We stick to the back roads, nothing risky. Recon element, you know our route home. Push out two miles ahead of us and come up on the net if you see anything."

I turned to the old man and gave him a silent nod, to which he responded by completely enveloping me up in a bear hug, surprising me with his strength. He pushed me back, holding me at arm's length by my shoulders and smiled as he spoke.

"You take care of yourself, Brother. Follow your heart and the Lord will keep you safe. God bless you all for what you're doing."

"Thank you, Brother. Are you sure you and the rest of the Brethren don't want to come with us?"

"Nay. Our place is here. There are many more who need help, whether it be safety, shelter, food or comforting. We took the same oath, Brother. You are the Sheepdogs, we are the Shepherds. You keep the wolves at bay, and we'll get as much of the flock to safety as we can."

I didn't have any response, but knew he was right. A nod and another hug were all I could give, and after our embrace, I made my way back to the Bradley.

J-Lo moved to take the shotgun seat with me, and as I turned and looked at the back, I saw eight scared little faces staring back at me. It was all I could do to fake a big smile and try to put them at ease.

"Hey, guys," I said to them with a smile and a wave.

"My name's Rob, and I'll be your driver today. This here's J-Lo," I said, pointing at J-Lo who turned to give a wave and smile as well.

"Make sure you buckle your seat belts, it might be a bumpy ride. We'll be on the road for a few hours, so feel free to take a nap if you can."

I could see they were terrified. My heart dropped, as I thought about my own kids back at our compound.

"You're safe now, guys. My friends and I have been doing this a long time and we're very good at what we do. There are lots of kids where we're going, and you can all play together once we get there."

One of the little girls got a smile on her face, and as I gave my biggest smile back to her, I heard Bulldog come over the radio.

"Truck one, moving."

I turned around, made sure my seat belt was fastened and started moving. I said another silent prayer as we exited the parking structure, praying we would make it back with all of these kids safely.

We miraculously made it all the way home in about two hours without any issues, and I let out a huge sigh of relief when I drove the Bradley through the front gates to our compound.

Thankfully, we had been smart to make extra spots in our underground garage in the event we were lucky enough for battlefield recovery of vehicles, and as I pulled into one of our parking spots and shutdown the engine, I heard a half-dozen quiet snores coming from the rear compartment.

J-Lo and I turned to find our young passengers passed out and sleeping on each other's shoulders. I kept the rear compartment closed so the sound of the other incoming vehicles wouldn't startle or wake them, and as I stepped out of the Bradley, several adults jumped down from the back of the deuce and a half truck and ran towards us.

They slowed a bit as I put my finger to my lips in the sign of silence and walked to greet them.

"Are they ok?" a distraught mother asked.

"Yeah, they're fine. They're all asleep back there."

"Hell, they were asleep the second we started moving," laughed J-Lo.

I could see the wave of relief on each of their faces and could only imagine how they felt.

As a father myself, I knew how hard it would be to be separated from your children for a drive like this through a combat zone.

But as a soldier, I knew that if we had gotten ambushed en route, it would be easier to control the situation. Scared parents don't listen to logic in those kinds of situations and can only think about their kids, which could end up getting us all killed.

Before we could say anything else, Chris made his way over to our group to give us the word.

"Josh wants everyone in the top house, five minutes."

"The kids are all sleeping in the back," J-Lo answered him.

Chris, a loving father himself, paused for a moment.

"Look, we don't know you guys," he said, facing the parents around us. "We can't just leave you down here by yourselves with our vehicles. I'm sure you understand. If you need help carrying the kids up, Rob will be happy to help."

Chris shot me a glance before he turned to walk out of the garage, letting me know he wasn't too pleased with me at the moment.

"So what do we do now?" asked one of the fathers standing around us.

"We do exactly what he said; you'll learn pretty quickly that's the best way to go about your life around here," J-Lo answered.

I started back towards the driver's hatch of the Bradley.

"I'll open the back. Let's try to be as quiet and gentle as we can, but we need to get up top - sleeping kids or not."

Walking into the living room with someone's sleeping daughter resting her head on my shoulder, I could see the rest of the newcomers sitting on the couches, chairs and anywhere they could fit.

Chris was in the middle of the large open living room, waiting on us to begin. Not knowing what to do with the little one, I found a place to stand and waited for his command.

"Ok, everyone, listen up," he started with his loud, commanding voice.

"It's late, so I'll keep this short. There are rooms with beds upstairs. The closets down here have extra sheets, blankets and sleeping bags. We weren't expecting visitors tonight," Chris said, shooting me an angry glance before continuing. "But thankfully, we have enough for everyone. The bathrooms and showers all work up here but we have a lot of people, so use the water sparingly. The pantry has some food, but remember we're in a survival situation here, so don't waste anything."

He looked around the room to ensure everyone got the point before continuing.

"The sun should be up in a few hours. Get some rest, and we'll come up and get you in the morning and introduce you to everyone else. Any questions?"

A tall, dark-haired man sitting on one of the couches raised his hand and spoke.

"Where are you guys going?"

"You don't need to know that just yet, just know we'll be close. The phones here connect directly to lines where we'll be, so if you need us before we're back here, you can use those. Anything else?" Looking around the room at the tired faces, it was obvious everyone just needed some rest.

"Get some sleep, we've got a lot of work to do tomorrow. Team, be in the team room in five."

With that Chris turned to leave, and I nodded to the mother of the little girl I was carrying that I was taking her upstairs. She followed me slowly as I climbed upwards, still weighed down by my armor and the little girl. She stood silently and watched as I laid her daughter gently on one of the beds.

When I turned to walk out of the room, she caught my arm and said, "Thank you. Please tell your friends that I said thank you and God bless you. All of you."

"Don't thank me yet, lady" I replied. "We've still got a long road ahead of us. Get some sleep, take care of your kids and we'll see you in the morning. We've all got kids of our own here. We'll introduce them in the morning so hopefully they can take their minds off this and feel a little normal."

I started feeling the aches and pains in my body as I walked back down the stairs and out into the cold Colorado night. The adrenaline was finally starting to slowly course through my veins, and as I made my way to the team room, I looked up at the stars and said a quick thank you to the heavens for bringing us home safely.

The guys were seated around the team room when I walked in and Chris immediately let his feelings off his chest as I began to strip off my body armor and lay it against the wall.

"What the hell, Rob?" he shouted at me. "As if we didn't have enough on our plates already?"

"Easy, Chris," answered Bulldog.

"Hold on," Chris continued. "We made this place for our families and us. We've got enough food and supplies to last us for a few months, but what are we going to do with all of these extra mouths to feed?"

"More importantly," Griz interjected, "how do we know these people are safe? We haven't vetted a single one of them! How do we know there isn't a mole up there reporting what each of us looks like and exactly where we are right now?"

The whole room turned and looked at me, displaying a mixture of emotions on their faces.

"What's our mission here, guys?" I asked, looking around the room.

"Take our country back," answered Chris angrily.

"So what's our country without her people?" I replied.

I let it settle in for a second, and hearing no responses, I stated my case.

"We're not going to save our country through combat operations alone. What's our motto? De Oppresso Liber, right? To free the oppressed. Those people up there are pretty damn oppressed right now, but besides that, they're Americans. Sure, it's our job to find, fix and destroy the enemy. But it's also our job to help our fellow Americans in any way we can."

"He's right," added Bulldog.

"If those were any of our families up there, we'd hope that someone would do the same for us. And to look on the bright side, we may have more mouths to feed now but we also have more people to help support this place while we're running missions. And,

Griz, the enemy hasn't been on the ground long enough to have sources, so I wouldn't worry about that."

I looked around the room for some support, and Josh chimed in.

"He's got a point. With the small number of operators we have in this room we can't be working on our facilities all day, manning the guard towers and running missions every night. We'll run ourselves ragged in a few days. At least now there are some extra hands to do a little work around here while we focus on the fight."

Chris clenched his jaw, but nodded in accordance.

"If any of these newcomers compromise us or get our families hurt, it's on you, Rob," he said.

I nodded at Chris, acknowledging his worries. There was no use arguing or trying to drive my point home any further. I knew deep down he understood, but his undying loyalty to his family and the team came before anything or anyone else.

"Good," added Bulldog. "It's late, and we're all tired. We'll have some explaining to do to our families in the morning, so let's get these guns cleaned and ready so we can get some rest."

"J-Lo and Tattoo, go get the big guns on the trucks refitted and ready to go back out," Josh directed.

"Chris, Buckeye and Ray, go take a look at those boxes we got on the deuce and a half. Get a good inventory, but most importantly, make sure we didn't bring any kind of tracking devices home in the boxes or on our new vehicles."

With that, everyone started moving on their priorities of work. We were all tired and sore, but knew that making sure we were ready to go again at a moment's notice took precedence over anything.

As I sat down to start cleaning my weapons, Bulldog came over and took a seat across from me with his rifle.

"Rob," he started, "I understand what you did. I get it. And I fully support your reasoning. But..."

He looked up to make sure I was looking him in the eyes and taking in his message.

"Chris has a very good point. I've got a wife and kids of my own here, as does everyone else. Don't you EVER pull a stunt like that again without clearing it through me or Josh, Roger?"

"Roger that, sir," I replied, looking him in the eyes and nodding.

"Chris will cool down once he gets some rest and we start putting the newcomers to work, and I suggest you steer clear of him until morning. He's just looking out for us...you know that."

"Understood," I answered.

As the two of us sat silently, cleaning our weapons, we began to hear the joking and ribbing at each other start up around the room from the rest of the team. Griz started making fun of Chad, Chad started making fun of Matty, Matty started making fun of Adam, and Tony started making fun of everyone.

By the time we were finished cleaning our weapons, the whole room was smiling and laughing just like the good old days.

With guys like this, we knew there was nothing that could stop us. And with 022 back together and operational again, the enemy had bought themselves more trouble than any nation or army could ever handle.

CHAPTER 7

BUILDING AN ARMY

The next morning came early and I felt aches and pains that I hadn't in ages.

Being underground killed most of your natural senses; the circadian rhythm and your body waking you up at first light were completely gone, but we had our own alarm clocks: kids.

Although Robert and Avery were still on California time, once they heard the other children running past our room and laughing and playing up and down the hall, they were up and ready to join the fun.

Robert jumped out of bed before I could change him out of his pajamas, and after I rolled over to try and get some more sleep, I knew it would be a futile attempt.

After a long and protracted pause at the edge of my bed, letting the soreness fade from carrying body armor and my muscles soaking up the adrenaline of the night before, I slipped on my flip flops.

I stepped out into the hallway as a flurry of waist-high hair and freckles ran past me, followed by a dozen laughing and screaming kids.

"Whose kids are these?" J-Lo asked, laughing at me from down the hall.

"I think they all came out of a petri dish I left open in the green house. I'll have to investigate after I get some coffee."

Walking into the kitchen I found most of the team sitting around, nursing mugs of coffee and looking like the tired zombies we were. I poured myself a cup and took a seat next to Corey and across from Bulldog, who smiled and winked at me.

"Well, Rob, congratulations. Now some of the wives love you for giving the kids something to keep them busy, and the other ones hate you for the extra headache."

"Is the split at least 50/50?" I asked with a grin.

"I'd say more around 70/30, but the good news is that it's in your favor."

"I'll take those odds any day. I take it the newbies are up and about?"

"Most. Some of the men got a little restless and woke up looking for things to do this morning. They want to pitch in and make sure we don't see them as just extra mouths and bellies to feed around here. And a few of them actually seem to have some skills we can use.
I think we found a carpenter up there, so that's a good start."

I looked around the room, noticing Chris wasn't around.

"Did the big guy have anything to say this morning?"

"He's up top, playing with the boys. His wife is a big part of the 70 percent, and they're having fun with the kids. You know him - once he's around kiddos he turns into a big teddy bear."

"Well I'll take that as a win then. Somebody put one up on the scoreboard for me."
Bulldog began to stand up as he gulped down the rest of his coffee.

"Speaking of scoreboards, we need to get back upstairs, AAR [After Action Review] and figure out what we do next. Team room in ten minutes."

Bulldog exited the room and everyone followed suit, finishing their mugs and washing them off in the sink before leaving the room.

As they did, Griz came over and punched me in the shoulder while I took the last gulps of my own, forcing me to spill a bit on my chest.

"Dude, that was my date shirt."

"Rob, if that was your date shirt then you're never getting laid ever again."

"Well I'm lucky somebody slept with me the two times. I've got the rugrats to prove it."

"Yeah right. They look a lot more like Ray than you anyway. We all have our doubts," he joked. "In all seriousness, sorry about getting on you last night. Good call...we could use some more numbers around here, and as much as I hate to say it, it was the right thing to do."

"Thanks, Brother, I really appreciate that. It felt right...I just hope it works out."

As we made our way into the hallway to head for the team room, the flurry of laughter and children ran past us again.

"Yeah, Bro, I think it will," Griz said as he smiled at me.

As the two of us walked up the stairs outside, I saw Chris buried in a pile of boys he was wrestling with.

"Team house in five" Griz yelled to him.

Chris stood up in a wave of kids, some still clinging to him and some falling into a heap of laughter as he rose.

"Roger," he yelled back to Griz, then shot a nod and a wink to me.

Some guys had to spend hours on the phone or over drinks to make amends; guys like us just needed a nod and everything was good.

Back in the team room, Bulldog and Josh were already at the front of the room, with the team scattered around in their regular seats.

As Chris walked in and closed the door behind him, Bulldog signaled that it was time to start and everyone immediately sat up in their chairs and stopped talking amongst themselves.

"Okay, men, let's start from the beginning," Bulldog said looking at everyone around the room.

"First things first, good job last night. We didn't have much time to plan, get settled or get situated, but we knew that target would only be open for a short time until they got set up, so kudos to everyone for being flexible and moving out. Matty, give us the recon play-by-play."

"Yes, sir." Matty replied and stood up in his spot.

"We identified a few good places to set in on the maps, and possible routes for the main force to infil if the roads had enemy traffic. We moved out and took the back roads to our positions, and called in to you as soon as we were in place."

"Good, Josh, can you walk us through the main assault force?"

"Well, we got the call from the recon element letting us know they were in place, had eyes on target and that our primary route was cleared hot. We moved in to assault the airport, cut the fence and started our attack. We got in and came under enemy fire as soon as we began shooting, and somewhere along the way, the ground opened up and soldiers began fighting with us. What the hell was that all about?"

Bulldog stepped in. "We'll get to that one at the end. I don't know what that was, but I suspect it will just be a distraction right now."

"Ok," Josh continued. "So as soon as our reinforcements from GI Joe Space Command started their assault --"

Sudden laughter broke out throughout the room and Josh let out a chuckle before continuing.

"Our surprise reinforcements immediately gave us the upper hand. It seemed like the enemy expected that about as much as we did. And that gave us enough time to do a little battlefield recovery."

He looked around the room and pointed to me and Buckeye before saying, "We went in there with three trucks, but as soon as we had the chance, these two scored us a Bradley and a deuce and a half, complete with booze, bullets and some kind of Russian MREs."

Bulldog stepped in again.

"Now, Rob, you still have some explaining to do, so why don't you cover the exfil."

"Roger, sir. We got in our trucks and thankfully they all started up, and after the recon elements set off their charges, we made our way out of there. Exfil was clean, and the GI Joe Space Command was still fighting as we were pulling off the objective."

Looking around the room, I knew what came next and could tell they were eagerly awaiting an explanation.

"So we chose to avoid the highways and drove through Denver to take another route back home. Going through the city we made a short stop to pick up our new attachments and then made our way home without incident."

"Not so fast, hot sauce," Chris interjected. "I think we could use a little more detail on that one."

With all eyes on me, I tried to figure out how to explain what happened.

"Well, a few miles into the trip we drove past a Masonic Lodge, so I, uh, decided to turn around and go pay them a visit."

"How in the world did you know anyone would even be there?" asked Josh. "I was up those steps with you, Rob. How did you know someone would answer the door?"

I glanced around the room again, trying to find my confidence and figure out how to explain my hunch.

"Well, I'm the only Mason here, and most of you probably only know what you've heard in conspiracy theories. The truth is, as Masons we are taught to live by certain Masonic principles, with Faith, Brotherly Love and Charity on the top of the list. After what we saw at the airport, I knew there were Masons out there fighting back."

"Hold the phone there, Rob," Jason said, pointing at me. "You know who those guys at the airport were?"

"You mean GI Joe Space Command?" I chuckled nervously.

"Yes, those guys. Do you know who they were?"

"Well, I didn't at first, but it clicked as we were on the drive home."

"Dude, stop waiting for us to ask questions!" Adam exclaimed, throwing his hands up. "If you know what the hell is going on here, spill the beans."

"Well, like I said, it was just a hunch. Have any of you heard the conspiracy theories about Denver International Airport?"

I was met by blank faces burning a hole through me, waiting for me to elaborate.

"Okay, so there are a lot of conspiracy theories about DIA. I know none of you pay attention to that stuff, and none of you are Masons, so probably none of you noticed walking through there that that place is full of Masonic imagery. There's even a cornerstone with a Denver Lodge's name on it - the Lodge we stopped at."

I looked around the room again, searching for any glimmer of understanding of what I was alluding to.

"Have any of you heard of DUMBs? Deep Underground Military Bases?" I asked.

Again, I was met with a room full of blank stares.

"Alright, here goes...hold on to your seats, boys. The conspiracy theories go that Denver International Airport was one of many Deep Underground Military Bases built around the country. Some said that they were all military, some said Freemason bases for the apocalypse. They're supposed to be completely sustainable fallout shelters able to withstand a nuclear blast and keep thousands of people alive for quite some time."

I paused, scanning the room again.

"Are you freaking kidding me? Am I seriously the only one here who's heard of this stuff?"

Griz shrugged and gave me a "whaddaya-gonna-do" look.

"That's all I know. That there are a ton of Masons in the military, a lot of military bases here in Colorado, and a lot of Masons here as well. So...who knows...maybe the conspiracy theorists actually had one right."

"So you're saying those soldiers were Masons?" asked Chad.

"That I can't say. It all happened so fast. None of them were wearing patches, but they all had US Military uniforms. Again, I don't know. I'm just trying to connect the dots of what I *do* know, but whoever they were, I suggest attempting to get in contact with them."

"Okay, that's about all I can handle of that for one day," said Bulldog.

"We can guess and conjecture later, but for now let's try to figure out where we go from here, especially with our new friends upstairs."

Tony stood to give his piece of mind.

"We always knew our numbers would make being here pretty rough. Like Bulldog said this morning, we know some of them have useful skills. Let's put those guys to work building more structures, train the others to pull guard and have the women pitch in with the gardens and anything else they can do around here."

Josh looked around the room at the heads moving slightly up and down in agreement.

"That sounds like a plan to me. When do we start?"

"No time like the present," added Chris.

"I say we get the men in here now, make sure we can trust them and start dividing up the tasks. Figure out who can work, who can shoot, and whether or not we can trust them all. If we're going to disrupt the enemy network we need to keep on them as much and as often as we can, so we don't have any time to waste."

"Well said," replied Bulldog. "Chris, Tony, get the men and bring them in here. Everyone else help me put these maps away until we know we can trust our new-found friends."

As Tony and Chris returned with the men, we quieted down and allowed them to introduce themselves. It turned out we had six total - a good number - and by the looks of them, they were at least in decent to pretty good physical shape.

The first in line was Jacob, a dark-haired man of average height and build who had prominent Jewish facial features. We were glad to learn that not only was Jacob a carpenter, but he was also a former Army reservist, and had some familiarity with most of our weapons.

Next up was a man built like a wrestler with a high-and-tight haircut who introduced himself as Bryan. Bryan was an insurance salesman now, but had been a Marine Infantry officer in Iraq and had served in the battle of Fallujah.

"Can you still shoot?" Josh asked as soon as he told us about his experience.

"I can shoot the nuts off a moving mosquito at 500 yards without a scope," was his reply.

As the room laughed, Josh asked him to stand off to one side, exclaiming that he would be part of the hunters.

The following man to introduce himself was Taylor, a tall redhead built like a brick shithouse. He owned a construction company and told us that he knew his way around the equipment as he doubled as the foreman on all of his projects.

"Do you have your own equipment?" asked Corey, who had been in construction before he came to the Army.

"Yes, sir." Taylor replied. "As far as I know, it's all still in our yard outside the city, locked up in a warehouse on my property."

Corey shot a glance to Bulldog. "I suggest that being one of our first missions."

"Good idea," replied Bulldog. "But how do we get it back here?"

"Well, I've got a flatbed we can use to transport the big stuff," answered Taylor.

Bulldog nodded and filed that away in his brain as Josh asked Taylor to stand off to the side opposite Bryan, telling Jacob to join him in our "worker" group.

As Taylor stood to one side, a man who was a bit shorter than Taylor but built like a heavyweight boxer was next in the introductions. He told us his name was John and that he owned a fancy steakhouse named JZ Williamson's in downtown Denver.

"Jesus," Ray exclaimed. "That's our favorite place. You guys make the best damn steaks in the country! My wife and I go there every month."

"Yup, that's the place."

"As I remember, you guys also have some serious top shelf booze, especially bourbon."

"I'm actually a bourbon expert," replied John. "I pride myself on our collection of bourbon and cigars, and before you ask, yes, it should still be locked up in the restaurant."
Ray shot an eager glance at Bulldog.

"Take it easy, Ray. Beans and bullets first, then we can focus on booze."

"Actually, sir," John spoke up. "I see that you guys have some generators around here. We do a lot of catering for high-end corporate events, and I just got a supply of food before the bombs started going off. We own a deep freezer that could be loaded on Taylor's flatbed and brought here. We could hook the deep freezer up to a generator and store more food than anyone here could eat in a year."

He looked at Ray before adding, "And the bourbon."

"That's what I'm talking about, Airborne," Chris laughed from the back of the room. "This guy just got my vote as most useful."

"Okay, John, please stand over there with Jacob and Taylor. We'll figure out logistics later.
And no, Ray, the booze storage isn't in your room."

Our next introduction came from a man the same height as John but about twenty pounds lighter named Mike. When Mike introduced himself as a local musician he was met with laughs and catcalls, but wisely followed it up with good news.

It turned out Mike was also an avid hunter who owned land that he hunted on several times a week. He quickly informed us that he had a huge store of ammo, reloading equipment and rifles at his house.

"But are you actually any good at hunting?" asked Griz.

"I haven't bought meat from a store in ten years and I eat steaks every night, so yeah...you could say I'm pretty decent."

Josh and Bulldog thought for a second before Josh pointed him to join Bryan in the hunter group.

At last, the final man stepped up and introduced himself as Jason.

He was another tall man with a short, military style haircut and a deep southern accent. Jason immediately proved himself as a useful addition to our group, having grown up on a proper ranch, spending his career in the Navy as a small arms instructor and retiring to a ranch here in Colorado with his family.

"Okay, that's great and all, but we can't have two Jason's here. And I came first, so what's your name gonna be?" asked Jason jokingly.

"Tex" shouted Chad, and from that point on, it was so.

Bulldog took a long look at our crew and mentally sized up our new additions.

"Ok, guys, nice to meet you all. We've got some things to talk about, so if you head back to the house we'll be with you in a few minutes."

With head nods all around, the men each looked around the room, seeming to have just as little of an idea about what would come next as we did. Taylor was the first to start heading for the door, and as it closed behind them, Bulldog and Josh moved to the front of the room.

"Alright, guys, so what's our next step?" asked Josh from his position at the head of the room.

"We've got to vet them," replied Corey from the corner.

"Right, but does anyone know how to go about doing that?" asked Bulldog.

"We don't exactly have an NSA database here to check their background or credit history, and we can't go around calling their references."

"I know what to do," answered Chris.

"I'm going to need everyone's help here because we're gonna to have to go old school. I'll form a matrix on each one of these guys, and we'll keep it somewhere they'll never see it."

"What kind of matrix?" asked J-Lo.

"It's pretty simple, really. Most of you have seen it in cheesy police tv shows or movies. We get a piece of butcher-block paper for each of these guys and put their picture in the middle.

Ask them about their life and history, and every time you finish a conversation with them, come back and give me any intel you learn, and we'll plot it on their matrix."

"Won't that be a dead giveaway? I mean, won't they know exactly what we're doing?" asked
Adam.

"It doesn't matter," Josh said from the front of the room.

"If they have something to hide, there are only two possible outcomes. One, they'll give us all the same exact canned answer, which will show up immediately. Or, they'll slip up and give different details during one of the dozen renditions they give about their life. Either way, we're just looking for rote repetition of a cover story or an inconsistency. It's that simple."

"And is that a surefire way to root out a mole or someone we don't want around?" asked Griz.

"That's the first part," responded Chris.

"The next step is to give them a set of circumstances for which we know the outcome. Basically, we become bait."

Bulldog spoke up from the front again.

"A few of them gave us intel about places we can go get supplies that we desperately need. If they were moles, that would be the worm on the hook for us, and the enemy knows it. So, we need to start planning missions to go get the food John told us about and construction equipment Taylor told us about."

"Don't forget the booze," piped Ray from his titled-back chair at the desk.

"Yes, Ray, and the booze. We'll plan missions to go get both, but we choose to pick up one, and then just send recon out to watch the second. We tell all the guys that we're going to both targets, and even leave to pretend we're going to the second. If enemy moves in to ambush us on the second, we know we have a mole. If not, we have a battlefield recovery."

"And steaks and booze," said Ray, almost tipping himself over in his chair as he reclined perilously far back.

"Yes, Ray," Bulldog laughed, "and booze."

"But our first step needs to be testing these guys to figure out who we can take on missions, who's a good enough shot to man our security, and who can help us out around the compound," Josh added.

Pointing at J-Lo and Tattoo, he gave the first order of business.

"We got some ammo and weapons from the objective last night, so let's take these boys shooting, see who can shoot and who we need to keep away from weapons unless absolutely necessary."

"Roger," came their replies.

"And you heard Chris. Everyone's job is to get to know these guys, and report back every time you leave a conversation with them. We need to know exactly what story they give each and every one of us so we can analyze. Let's get Taylor and John in here, find out where they keep their stuff so we can start planning."

"I'm on it," yelled Jason as he headed out the door.

"Bravos, take everyone else to the range. Let's see what we're dealing with here."

Once Bulldog and Josh had the coordinates to Taylor's warehouse and John's restaurant plotted on the map, we set to planning our next mission.

It was a pretty easy decision; with Taylor's construction company located outside of the city and John's restaurant smack in the middle, it would be safer and easier to get Taylor's equipment and send the Raven over John's restaurant to check for a potential ambush.

After a few hours of planning our routes and actions, the Bravos reported back that it had been a pretty good day at the range. According to J-Lo, they were all decent shots, but Bryan and Mike were the shining stars.

Once we had all of the planning complete and sensitive items hidden, we called the new group back into the team house. Josh took the lead laying out the plan.

"We've got more people here now than we planned for, so sustaining this many is going to take some work. Taylor, we could use your stuff to help build onto our infrastructure, and John, we could use the extra food."

Chris stepped in to brief our routes.

"Your construction warehouse is located right here," Chris said, pointing with a yardstick to a location about thirty miles northwest of us.

"That's going to be our first target. We'll take a few trucks so people can get out to drive and guard the flatbed, then we'll move on to John's restaurant for the food."

"And booze," added Ray.

"Food and booze, right!" snickered Chris.

"Isn't that a little dangerous to drive around and do all of that in one fail swoop?" asked Jacob.

"It is," replied Bulldog. "But time is of the essence. We already hit a major target last night, and since Denver is such a big area and DIA is the largest airport around here, it'll probably be their center of operations for this region. I don't know how long we'll get until that place is completely locked down, so if we're going to go, it has to be soon."

"How soon?" asked Tex.

"Tonight," answered Josh, looking around the new group.

"No sense in sitting around waiting. We'll pull out of the gate at midnight tonight, which should put us back here by first light."

"So what do we do?" asked Mike. "Are we coming with you?"

"Half are, half are staying back with some of our guys. We could use the help back here guarding the compound so we can take more of our team with us," answered Josh.

"Mike, Taylor and John, you guys are coming with us," Tattoo spoke loudly from the side of the room.

"Mike was one of the best shots. And Taylor and John, we'll need you to help us get your stuff."

The three new men nodded their heads up and down in affirmation.

"So what do we do?" asked Mike again.

Tony threw in an answer from his chair. "If you see us start shooting, shoot in the same direction. That's about it. Oh yeah, and don't shoot us."

"What do the rest of us do?" asked Jacob.

"While the guys are gone on the mission, we still need to guard this base, so we'll put you into the guard roster with our guys so they can explain what to do. And while you're not on guard, we'll take you around the compound and talk about what we need to do to keep this place running," answered Chris.

As much as he hated it, Chris knew he'd be staying back from missions for a few days, not only to build the intelligence matrix but also to ensure that if everyone on the mission died, someone would still be left to lead.

"So let's get our gear on," Bulldog commanded.

"We leave here in an hour. J-Lo and John will issue you guys armor, ammo and weapons, and when we meet at the trucks, Josh will tell you which one to ride in."

"And don't shoot us," Tony reiterated from his chair.

"So meet at the trucks in an hour?" asked Taylor.

"You're on military time now, bud" Bryan interjected.

"Always be fifteen minutes early. If you're only ten minutes early, you're late."

Everyone from the team looked on at Bryan and grinned.

"We just might have to keep this guy," joked Griz, as the room erupted in laughter.

We were standing in a circle by the garage forty-five minutes later, gear on, weapons locked and loaded and truck engines idling as Josh started our convoy brief.

While we knew that the mission would start split operations and send one team back after securing Taylor's construction equipment until we could get eyes on to the restaurant, Josh gave the brief as if we'd be rolling straight from one target to the next.

While the three additions coming with us weren't exactly a huge jump in our numbers, it was enough to add another vehicle to our convoy.

This meant we could get Taylor's equipment, shift one person to drive the flatbed and still have two trucks to escort it back and another truck, plus the Bradley, to proceed onto John's restaurant if it wasn't a trap.

We each moved to our respective locations as Josh pointed out vehicle assignments, and as soon as we heard the command "let's roll" from Bulldog, the trucks started out of the underground garage.

I was driving the Bradley which meant I had the lead due to its extra firepower, and with Ray up top, I felt about as safe as I ever could.

We each had our own personalities, and while Ray could sometimes be extremely over the top with his joking and laughing, when it came down to business, he was stone-cold serious. I couldn't think of anyone else I'd rather have watching my back as we drove into battle.

We were still less than a week into the invasion and had no idea what the enemy troop levels were. Thankfully, it seemed they didn't have enough ground troops or air power to effectively patrol anything outside of the major cities yet, which meant the back roads we drove to Taylor's warehouse were dark and empty.

Knowing we'd be outnumbered in almost any case, it was best to stay completely off the grid if possible.

We took the "scenic route," driving along back roads from our compound until we were about twenty minutes outside of Denver, and then took an extra-wide berth outside of the city limits towards the first objective, doing whatever we could to ensure we'd stay off the enemy's radar.

As we drew closer to the objective, Josh came over the radio from his truck behind me.

"Taylor says we're getting pretty close. Nothing's coming up on the Blue Force Tracker so stop in the driveway and we'll let him to unlock the gates."

"Roger!" I answered into my radio.

"Truck three, go a hundred meters down the east road and keep a lookout. Truck four, go west and watch us back there. Keep your lights off and trucks running. I'll call you guys when we're in."

"Roger," came the replies from the other vehicles' occupants.

As I drove the Bradley off the main road and along the dirt and rock driveway, I began to see a pretty substantial piece of property - much more than Taylor had led us to believe.

I stopped the Bradley ten feet shy of the gate and could hear Ray scanning the area with the heavy guns as Taylor made his way to unlock it.

While I had expected nothing more than a cattle gate around a tiny property with some scattered junk equipment, the gate Taylor was unlocking was twenty-foot-high wrought-iron fencing.

I used my night vision goggles to view massive warehouses, cranes, bulldozers and other mechanical dinosaurs littering the property in the darkness.

He had to put all of his weight into it, but after Taylor swung the gates open, he turned around and waved us in.

"Stay alert," I turned around and said up to Ray before I depressed the throttle to begin our movement into the compound.

"Stay alive," Ray replied, reverting back to the old saying we learned so well in Infantry basic training.

"Jeez, would you look at that!" Buckeye said into his radio as we slowly moved along and my night vision goggles shone an eerie green illumination of the brand-new rows of massive machinery parked around the property.

"He says to pull into this building straight ahead of us, the one-story concrete one. That's where the keys are," directed Bulldog over the radio.

I pulled the Bradley to the far side of the building and parked so we could cover anything coming at us from the back half of the property, and Bulldog called out over the radio for the other trucks to come in.

As Ray stayed on the gun and continued to scan the area for threats, I dismounted the vehicle but kept the engine running in case we needed to make a sudden exit. Walking in the door just after Taylor stepped inside and turned on the lights, I began to understand the true scope of his "little business."

Just like any military planning room I'd ever spent time in, most of the walls inside his office were lined with all sizes of white dry-erase boards, each filled with project data, timelines, projections and other important information.

Any area on the walls that wasn't filled with whiteboards was covered with pictures of projects in various states of completion, ranging from average-sized houses to the roof being assembled on a new baseball stadium.

As I marveled at the feats of engineering and manpower, I heard a whistling sound behind me as Corey walked in and made it well known he was impressed.

"This is all yours?" he asked, looking at Taylor.

"Well, I can't take all the credit. My dad started this company, did all the real heavy lifting to get it off the ground, hired the good crews and formed the relationships that landed most of my big contracts. He built the machine and I just keep it going."

"Uh, I worked in construction and owned my own construction company between stints in the Army, dude. Don't be modest. This is amazing."

"Thanks," Taylor replied, shifting on his feet and looking around the room, obviously not one to easily take a compliment.

"So based on what we'll need back at the compound, I say we take these two flatbed tractor trailers," he said, walking over to a wall of well-organized keys, each one labeled with number-letter combinations stenciled on the wall.

"That way we can load a forklift, bobcat and backhoe on one, and take the other to John's to pick up his storage containers."

"How long until they're on the truck and ready to rock?" asked Bulldog as he walked into the room and began to survey the information scattered around the walls.

"I have a crane specifically for loading equipment, so fifteen minutes max and we can roll out. Also, I don't know how much fuel you guys keep, but I've got my own tanks here. Not sure how we can move them though."

"No time for the tanks now," answered Buckeye as he strolled into the office.

"But if you have any smaller fuel containers, we could use them. If we can set the tanks aside somewhere on the compound we would be able to set up a place to take them, but we're not ready for them tonight and don't have the time."

"Got it." Taylor said, walking over to a large map on an adjacent wall and pointing.

"Here's our fuel point. The area is full of drums, and you guys can fill as many as you want for us to take back. We can put them on the flatbed with the equipment for now."

"On it," answered Buckeye before anyone else said anything.

"Matty and I will go start pumping while you guys load the equipment. Bring the flatbeds over when they're filled up and we'll load the fuel drums last."

A nod from Bulldog and Buckeye turned to walk out, stopping just shy of the door.

"It looks like you've been on some pretty big projects here. Did you guys do any city work for municipal buildings?" he asked Taylor.

"Sure. We did the reconstruction of city hall a few years back and have laid a lot of foundations for the work they've been doing over the past ten years."

"Still have the blueprints?" Buckeye asked.

"Of course," Taylor answered, walking over to a large wall of filing cabinets on the far side of the large office. "Anything in particular you want?"

"Anything that would either serve as a good command station, has reinforced concrete or a large basement or underground area that can control the water or power for an area. And of course, city hall."

"What are you thinking?" asked Corey.

"I'm thinking of creating a little chaos," Buckeye said, smiling. "Their generals need offices, they'll need ammo depots and, of course, water and power. If we know the layout of all of those areas, we can stack the deck in our favor."

As Taylor began using an iPad to identify different drawers containing blueprints of interest, Corey and I took them as he pulled them out. Buckeye left to grab Matty and start on the fuel, and in a few short minutes, we were loading the first of the equipment onto the massive flatbed.

Tattoo was seated in the back of his truck as I exited the building, illuminated by the glow of the screens he was watching. The guys put two Ravens up while we were inside, and Tattoo was currently guiding them to John's restaurant for the second half of the mission.

As Taylor, Corey and Tony began cinching down thick ropes and chains to hold the equipment in place, we got the word from Tattoo that the next objective was clear of enemy.

"How long can we keep those things on the objective?" asked Josh.

"We should have another two hours, no problem," answered Tattoo.

"Great, it's only about twenty minutes to get there, so let's get moving!" said Josh as he put his hand up and waved in a circle above his head in a round-up motion.

We each made our way to the vehicles, and after loading the fuel drums on the flatbed, made our way back out of the compound. We stopped outside as Taylor locked the massive gates behind us.

As soon as everything was just as we'd found it again, the trucks began to pull away. We were going into split-team operations, which added a bit of danger with decreased numbers, but increased the chances of getting our new bounty home.

As two trucks headed south protecting the flatbed full of our new equipment, we started moving north with another flatbed of our own, on our way to John's restaurant in the heart of the city to pick up storage containers, food, and of course, booze.

We knew booze would be needed for our morale, and planned accordingly during our preparations. Several of us made decent homemade wine, and Ray even made a pretty good beer. But it would be nice (and useful for trade) to take anything we could get our hands on now.

Had this been any other mission in any of our pasts, we would place a Quick Reaction Force [QRF] staged somewhere close enough to reach us if we got into serious trouble.

Here, we just didn't have the manpower or vehicles, so once we said goodbye to the other convoy, each convoy was on its own.

Moving northeast and farther into the city now, I could sense my muscles tensing and heard Ray as he became more and more anxious with his movements, trying to cover as much area as possible to ensure no one was going to get the drop on us.

Any invasion has to move in parts, segments or campaigns, taking as much territory as possible at a time. The basic idea is to take one area, secure it, set up logistics and operations, then move your troops farther out to secure more real estate.

As such, we knew our part of the region wouldn't be heavily patrolled quite yet, but the city was sure to be crawling with troops.

We knew that taking out the transport planes and runways at the airport slowed down their plans significantly, but without eyes on target we had no way to verify the results of that operation. Bulldog led the first convoy home, so Josh was commanding us now, and once we entered the heart of downtown he began barking out orders. Each of us were on edge, and it was becoming obvious.

While our mission here was a recovery operation, specifically going to recover food and equipment to sustain ourselves, we each knew that in the end this was a movement to contact and were prepared for an ambush to come at any time.

We were going into the lion's den, and whether or not we'd make it all the way back was anyone's guess. But for the idea of real steaks on our families' plates and bourbon in our bellies tonight, it was well worth the trip.

As we moved farther and farther into downtown, Josh came over the radio to guide us in.

"John says to take a right on this next street, pull into the alley on your immediate left and we'll go in through the back. That's where he has the storage units and a backdoor for loading."

"Got it. That looks kinda like a deathtrap to me though, what do you think, Josh?" asked Ray from the gunner's seat.

"I agree one hundred percent, but I also don't think there are too many other options. The only other place to park is out on the street, which would draw more attention to us. We'll keep both Ravens overhead and have a ten-minute window to be rolling out once we stop."

"I've got the Ravens over us now, and we look good," interjected Tattoo.

"Good. Tony and I will head up to the roof to provide overwatch and sniper cover. The rest of you act like pirates taking a ship - I want everything we can get in one move. Ray, you're in charge of getting the containers on the flatbed. Everyone else, go inside and grab everything you can."

As I brought the Bradley to a stop in the alley behind John's restaurant, Josh came over the radio once more.

"Ten minutes starts now - go!"

Before I was out of the truck, the back door was unlocked and John was throwing up the loading doors.

"Liquor is that way," he said pointing to the front. "And food is this way," he said, pointing to the right. "I'll grab the cooking equipment we need, you guys are welcome to whatever you can carry."

With everyone else tasked out, only Matty and I were left to carry the supplies, so we got to work. He followed John's directions to the food storage, while I made my way to the front for the booze.

The bar was nothing short of first-rate and quite massive. It put me in awe for a moment, realizing that I had carte blanche to grab whatever I wanted from a bar containing bottles worth more than I'd ever made in an annual paycheck.

After taking stock and controlling my urges, I analyzed the shelves from a medical perspective. Bourbon was great, but the higher alcohol content with low impurities stuff could be used to sterilize instruments, so I started with the vodka and even found a bottle of Everclear, though I was a bit unsure as to why that would be in such a high-class place as this.

I found some empty boxes and milk crates and began loading. Once I had all of the clear liquor I could carry, I started on the fun stuff: the bourbon and even a few bottles of champagne.

Knowing the seconds were ticking down, I did my best to hurry but found myself awestruck like a kid in a candy store. I figured beer would be of the least value for us, so decided to make that my last trip.

As I began carrying out my last load of bottles, Tattoo's voice came to life in my headphones.

"I've got movement over here. Do you guys see this?"

"Distance and direction?" replied Josh.

"1000 meters, North East. We've got a small convoy of three vehicles a few blocks over, no dismounts."

"We can't see them from here," answered Josh. "What are they doing?"

"They're doing a linear patrol, taking each block in order."

"Alright, guys, get in the trucks and prepare to move. Tony and I will stay up here until everyone's out. How we doing on those containers, Buckeye?"

"Locking the wenches down now, ready to roll, boss."

"Good. Gunners, get ready - it looks like they're coming right for us."

I ran back inside to get one more load of booze and a portable humidor of cigars, and walked out to find Griz standing with his rifle pointed at the back of John's head while John stood with his hands against the wall.

I stopped dead in my tracks.

"Dude, what are you doing?"

"This is what we expected, right? Either they'd be here waiting for us or they wouldn't. They're here, so we know this guy's a mole."

"Dude, that's just a random patrol. We've had eyes on this place for hours. If they were waiting for us, there would have been several companies of infantry swarming us as soon as we went inside."

"I'm not taking any chances. These guys keep driving, he keeps breathing. They stop--"

"That's a little much, dude. We need all the help we can get, Griz. Look at this, the back of the Bradley's full of prime steaks and bourbon. If he's a mole, he's the best damn mole I've ever heard of."

"Who gives a shit about steaks and bourbon, Rob? Those soldiers out there most likely killed all of my family back home and are trying to overtake your country. Steaks and bourbon or not, if this guy's a mole, his head is about to paint this wall."

I took a few steps over to Griz and put my hand on the barrel of his rifle to move it away from John's head.

"Back the hell off, Rob. What do you think you're doing?"

"Trying to stop you from doing something stupid, Griz. We need friends right now, and this isn't how you make friends."

"Screw friends. Are this guy's friends out there patrolling the street? Are his friends waiting to ambush us, go back to the compound to rape our wives and kill your kids?"

"I'm just saying let's give John here the benefit of the doubt, dude. Like I said, we've had eyes on this place for hours and--"

We both heard Josh's voice come to life in our headphones.

"Patrol's gone, they didn't even slow down. Looks like they're just patrolling the entire city and searching for anything."

Griz softened his glare and allowed me to push the barrel of his rifle all the way down.

"Roger," came Tattoo next over the radio. "Nobody in tow, no air anywhere. I pulled a little higher and it looks like there are small squads doing the same thing all over the city. Time for us to bounce."

"You heard the man, Rob, time to bounce." Griz growled, staring me dead in the eyes.

"I think we have time for one more load of booze, Griz, I didn't have any time to grab beer, but if you go to the bar I bet you can grab a keg or two while I put this stuff in the back of the Bradley."

"Do they have Guinness?"

"Bro, they even have local German Hefeweizen. Get you some, Brother!"

With that, I finally saw a grin from the corner of Griz's mouth, and after less than a second of hesitation, he turned and ran inside.

Walking up to John and patting him on the shoulder I told him to turn around.

The first thing that crossed my mind was how perfectly calm he was for a man who'd just had the barrel of an M4 pointed at the back of his head, execution style.

"You all right, dude?"

"Yeah, but what was that all about?" asked John, rubbing the back of his neck.

"We're all a little on edge. I've got my kids back at the compound, but haven't heard from my parents since the invasion. Most of the guys are the same way and, well, some show it a little more than others."

"So you're saying everyone thinks I'm a traitor?"

"No, not at all. But you have to understand your environment here. We've known each other for the better part of a decade. We've fought side by side in every bad part of the world, have lost friends together and have killed enemies together. You're stepping into the tightest circle of friends you could possibly imagine. So if anything goes wrong, those not yet in the circle will get blamed first."

"So don't screw up is what you're saying?"

"Yeah, not even that. There's no nice way to say this, but just know your place for a little while. My first piece of advice upon arriving to this team was to shut my mouth until they told me I was allowed to talk."

"And the second?"

"Buy a case of beer for the team. You just trumped me with steaks and bourbon for guys who were planning on living off MREs for the next few years, so I think you'll be ok. Just understand tensions are high, it's not personal, and we appreciate your help."

"Guns up, let's roll!" proclaimed Josh over the headphones as he and Tony exited the building, coming down from their sniper's perch.

"And speaking of place, your place now is back in the truck. Good haul, bro, you're going to be a very popular guy when we get back to the compound."

"Thanks, man. Why don't you ever say home? Your kids, friends and everything you own is there. Isn't that home?"

"That will never be home. My home is burning, and home is where the heart is. I don't have time for sentiments now. I'll find a new home when this is all over, but until then, the compound is where I'll hang my hat in between killing the people trying to destroy my country."

Tony popped my helmet with the palm of his hand as he walked past.

"You heard the man, let's get on the road. Daddy's hungry for some steaks!"

I looked back at John and shot him a wink.

"These are some of the best human beings you will ever meet, and are all my Brothers. Give them a reason to love you, and you'll be in. Give them a reason to hate you, and it will suck to be you."

I turned and walked toward the Bradley, putting my last box in the back and arranging the bottles to ensure we didn't lose any on the way back. Looking up in the gunner's nest, Ray was already cradling a bottle of choice Bourbon in his arms.

"Bro, do you know how much this bottle costs?"

"Right now it costs the ride home, because if you crack that bottle and miss an ambush or something, it'll never touch your lips."

Not getting the hint, he looked up at me with amazement in his eyes.

"They only make 100 bottles of this stuff a year. This bottle here is over $1,000 a glass, dude. Holy crap. I never thought I'd actually hold one of these."

"I tell you what, Ray. If you make sure we make it home tonight, that drinks on me."

Still not getting the joke, he carefully wrapped the bottle in the extra jacket he kept in his backpack and placed the whole package inside.

"Sorry, Rob, but I think this John guy is my new best friend. No hard feelings."

"None taken. But now you've got my interest, so if you two lovebirds drink that whole bottle together and don't save any for me, I'll be pissed."

I took my place back in the driver's seat and waited for the word to go. I watched Griz and Tony each roll a keg out of the loading dock as John closed and locked the doors.

If we ever wanted to come back and get a second helping here, we needed to make sure it didn't stand out. Any open doors just might invite the prying eyes of the enemy, and we didn't want that.

As Griz and Tony each cleaned and jerked their kegs into the back of the HUMVEE, Josh came back over the radio.

"Mount up. Let's take the alternate roads back. I don't want to run into one of these patrols right now - my mind is set on steak tonight and at this point I'm not leaving that flatbed, no matter what."

"Uh, that's great, Josh, remember I'm driving this thing. I would hope you wouldn't leave me - steaks or not," joked Buckeye over the radio.

"You know I love you, Bro, but this guy loves a rib eye more than any one of you, so let's get on the road. Lead the way, Rob. Ravens are overhead."

As a Texan who had been living in Southern California during medical school, it had been entirely too long since I'd sunk my teeth into a good piece of beef, and the steaks that night were like none I had ever tasted before.

John turned our little kitchen into a full-blown, five-star steakhouse, and for the night we weren't at war, but rather a bunch of friends sitting around eating and joking. The only reminder of our stark reality was taking turns to switch out the guys on guard duty so they could come eat as well.

I'm not sure if I was moved more by the wine before, the perfection of the salty, bloody steak and crispy, slightly charred asparagus, the bourbon and cigar afterward on the porch with the guys, or the fact I had been missing the team since the day I left them to head off to medical school.

But I couldn't stop smiling from the second I smelled John cooking the steaks to the last puff of my Hyde Park Macanudo cigar on the patio, drinking $1,000 a glass bourbon with Ray, Tony, Josh, Jason and John.

"What's up with you, Rob? You've been grinning at me like you want to get into my pants all night, dude," joked Ray.

I just smiled and shook my head from side to side as I looked at the group.

"I don't know, man, I just missed you guys."

"Oh, sweet baby Jesus. Are you gonna cry, Rob?" laughed Tony.

"Not quite yet, but if I don't get another glass of that bourbon stat I just might."

As the bottle was passed around the circle back to me, for the first time in as long as I could remember there was a moment of silence amongst the guys. As I poured my last glass for the night, I knew there was no other place in the world I belonged in more than right there, on that porch, with them.

CHAPTER 8

FIRST LOSS

I awoke to the sound of children laughing, playing and running up and down the hallway past our room. Avery was fast asleep but I saw that Robert's bed was hastily abandoned.

While everyone ate their fill of perfectly cooked steak the night before, only the adults took part in the post-dinner drinks. We may have been in the mood for a little extra rest that morning, but the kids felt like playing and weren't waiting for their parents to wake up.

Walking into the kitchen I found a steaming, half-empty carafe of coffee, indicating I wasn't the only adult up.

Poking my head back out into the hallway, I saw there weren't any other open doors (or movement, for that matter), so I decided to make my way up to the team house and find what was in store for the day.

Walking through the brisk, cool Colorado breeze was what my tired body and foggy brain needed. It had been an awfully long time (before med school as I remembered) since I'd stayed up late drinking with friends, and my head was making me pay the price.

While I may have forgotten just how much fun the bonding was, I definitely forgot how much the next morning slowed you down.

Opening the door and walking into the team house, it seemed as if I was the only one sleeping in. Bulldog was at the table looking over a map with a man I'd never seen before, wearing an Army uniform complete with Special Forces patches and tab, while Matty and Chad toyed with the PSC-5 radio in the corner.

Walking a little closer to nose-in on the conversation, Bulldog looked up and noticed me.

"Major, let me introduce you to Rob. He's one of our medics. Actually, he's a doctor, but he was a medic when we were on 022."

The new guy stood up straight, turned to face me and offered his hand. Looking at his uniform I first observed the rank of major on his chest.

He was about my height with short, dark brown hair, a piercing stare and a black, double-headed battle-axe fastened to his belt. He shook my hand with a vice grip of a shake and I couldn't hesitate being a smart ass.

"So, did we grow you in the basement or something? Where did you come from?" I asked.

The Major got a huge grin on his face and let out a mountain of a laugh.

"Actually, Bulldog and I here were hating our lives during command time and riding desks together when these guys decided to invade our country and give us something fun to do," he replied.

Bulldog got a smile on his face and interjected.

"The Major here leads a small group doing the same exact thing as us. Most of Special Forces knew something like this became inevitable with the political climate and economic turmoil our country fell into, and as it turns out, there are a few other teams who linked up and are taking the fight to the enemy."

"Is that why we haven't seen as many enemy troops as we'd expect in an invasion?" I asked both of them.

"Well, we're not seeing them here," answered The Major. "But they're all over the rest of the country. Funny as it may seem, the pockets of fiercest resistance are around Special Forces bases - here in Colorado, Washington State, North Carolina, Kentucky, Florida. Some of that may be attributed to the fact that most of those states also have avid hunters and didn't enforce the gun confiscation that the federal government tried to enact. But it's pretty uncanny when you look at the maps of where we're fighting back plotted against where the SF groups are located."

"How long until they figure that out and start nuking these areas?"

"Well, fortunately, it seems we have something they want. I was going to save this for when the entire team got here, but--" he stopped, looking up at Bulldog for approval, who nodded for him to continue.

"This isn't just a take-out-the-big-kid-on-the-block kind of invasion. They're here for our resources. We pissed off most of the world, our bankers bankrupted everyone, and when we bailed them out and destroyed the dollar, the people holding our debts decided our money was no good, but our oil, natural gas, minerals and such definitely were."

"So why are we seeing Hezbollah fighters? I know we can't possibly owe them anything."

"No," The Major replied, "they just had a chip on their shoulder, and when Russia and China decided to come in, they knew Hezbollah would be a cheap and easy way to start the offensive and not risk too many of their own men."

"China?" I asked. "We haven't seen any Chinese troops or equipment. Are you sure?"

"Who do you think took out our power and communications grids to start this whole thing off?" the Major questioned. "The second China realized we couldn't pay back the trillions of dollars we owed them, the wheels went into motion."

"Awesome. Any more good news for the day?" I joked.

"Actually, that's what I'm doing here. We have several resistance teams that are formed around this area, and we figured it would be good to start working together on a cohesive battle plan rather than just trying to pick off the enemy in small pockets."

"Like an all-out raid on their headquarters?"

"No, just a strategic initiative based on the skill sets of each team, their strengths and weaknesses."

"Rob, we're basically trying to create a plan to utilize resources the most efficient way possible, just like a company command would do when giving missions to its teams," Bulldog said.

"You guys, for example," said The Major, motioning around the room at our maps, enlarged pictures and graphics, "are a Special Reconnaissance team. You're better than most at getting in and gathering intel, figuring out the best area for advancing on an objective, attacking, and moving out without being caught."

"My team," he continued, "is more of a door-kicker team. We have another mobility team with a lot of vehicles including ATVs and things like that. We just want to make sure we're all doing what we do best to accomplish our mission."

Bulldog directed my attention to the map laid out in front of the two men.

"The Major is here to show us a layout of the enemy picture so far. I guess besides being door kickers, one of the guys on their team is some kind of NSA-level hacker that got into their mainframe as soon as they put up a network and got a map and battle plan of their activities."

Looking down I could assess the familiar markings denoting enemy unit size, strength and location. While it had been quite some time since I'd read this type of map, some things like the rectangle and X showing infantry troops never left my consciousness.

Zeroing in on our area to study which units were around us, I noticed a few symbols that I didn't remember ever seeing before. I immediately pointed them out to ask, and The Major laughed.

"That's what I'm here to talk to you guys about." Bulldog pointed to the three locations scattered throughout the region surrounding our compound.

"These are re-education camps. You can call them POW or concentration camps or whatever you like, but this is where they're taking the people they round up to put them in prison."

"Why are they all so close to us?" I asked.

"They're all over the country," The Major replied.

"But it seems as if this location was perfect for them for the same reasons you guys chose it for your compound - close enough to the city for access, far enough away to not be randomly happened upon unless someone knew what to look for and where."

"So what do we do?" I asked.

"That's entirely up to you," replied The Major.

"We're focusing our operations on disrupting their logistical supply routes on the north side of the city. You guys have more land here than most of the other groups, and since we don't know exactly how many friendlies or non-friendlies are on these camps, we figured it would be a prime mission for you to do some recon, figure it out and then hit the compound if you think you can pull it off."

The door opened behind me as the rest of the team began to file in. Apparently, I wasn't the only dirt bag who slept in this morning.

"Who the hell is this?" Tony exclaimed as he walked in.

"Leaving," replied The Major as he extended his hand for Bulldog and then me. "I'll be in touch. Your commo guys have our frequencies now, so anytime you need us, feel free to call. Watch yourselves out there, boys."

The Major turned and walked out of the room as the rest of the guys followed him with their eyes.

"Seriously, who the hell was that?" Tony asked, dumbfounded.

"An old friend. We've got a lot to talk about. Have a seat, men."

After filling in the rest of the team on the details, Bulldog began to lay out our next mission.

"We don't know how many, but we do know they're keeping Americans in these camps," he said, pointing to the three locations in our immediate area.

"By hitting these targets, we accomplish several of our missions: freeing Americans, demoralizing and destabilizing the enemy, and adding to our numbers."

"So where do we start?" asked Chad.

"We start with recon," answered Josh. "We have three potential targets here, but don't know anything about friendly or enemy numbers. We need to get eyes on and some pictures of these places so we can get a good idea of what we're dealing with."

"Why not just send the Raven over?" asked J-Lo.

"We're assuming they don't know we're close," answered Tattoo.

"The Raven is a great tool when people aren't looking for or expecting it, but if they happen to spot them flying over their base, they'll know we're somewhere close."

"Exactly. This needs to be a boots-on-the-ground, eyes-on-target type of mission so we can get the info we need without them knowing we were ever there," finished Josh.

"We'll send out three teams of two men each tonight. Each of you will have one of these bases as your objective, and we need to know everything about them. How many enemy troops, how many friendlies, how many entrances and exits, locations of the best entrance/exit routes to get in there... Also, what do we need? Can we hit one without the other two immediately coming to their aid?" added Bulldog.

"We've got four medics," directed Chris, "so you guys are all going out except, Rob."

I started to put up a fuss but Josh stopped me cold.

"We have to keep one of you guys around in case something bad happens to the others, and you've been out on every mission so far. You stay."

Josh went to the board and started writing names.

"Jason, you and Tony will be together on objective one. Corey, you and Tattoo on two. Adam, you'll be with Matty on three. Any questions?" Josh asked as he finished writing the last name and turned around.

"Good, then get to work. If you're staying back on this one, help these guys pack. If you're going out, get your stuff together and get some rest. This is going to be a long hump, we obviously can't roll there in the trucks if we want to go unseen. You guys can take the motorcycles and ATVs most of the way, but you'll still be walking in the last few miles and will need to circle the entire place on foot."

Chris stood up and added his piece. "We have a lot to do around here with our new construction equipment and the like. After you finish helping these guys pack, don't disappear. When they're packed and ready, we need to get to work. Come to me for your assignments and we'll get this place in shape."

As soon as Chris finished, the room became a flurry of activity. Recon was always a tough mission to pack and plan for. On one hand, you wanted to be as light as possible so you could move long distances quickly and undetected. On the other hand, with only a two-man team, you need to be ready to defend yourself should things go bad.

When the last of the bags were packed and the guys going out on the mission were back downstairs getting some shut-eye, the rest of us met back up in the team room, including the new additions.

With the new gear and supplies gained from the previous night, we had a lot of work to do to ensure they were put to good use. And with Taylor's equipment, the amount of improvements we could make on the compound was limitless.

Chris was quick to separate us into groups according to what we'd be doing for the rest of the day. I'd be leading the group that would be using the backhoe to create more plumbing for the restrooms and then moving on to increase our garden size substantially.

The Bravos would be taking our newcomers and teaching them more shooting drills, how to man a guard post, and weapons familiarization so they knew how to take care of them.

John, Ray and Buckeye would be moving our new cold storage units to a good location and hooking them up to the generators.

It was a hard day, but one that needed to be had. We knew this would be the eventual outcome of our mission, but at least there were a few more hands to pitch in now.

As we moved farther and farther out defending the country and taking the fight to the enemy, it was inevitable that we'd be required to increase our footprint and take on more people to assist us in the many functions required of a fighting force.

Jacob may have been a carpenter by trade, but he also turned out to be quite knowledgeable in plumbing, and what started out as a plan for a glorified slit trench soon became a full bathroom, complete with toilets and showers.

Ray was extremely thorough in his planning, and true to form as a packrat, stored plenty of piping to facilitate building anything our hearts desired.

The garden was a bit of a passion of mine; I had always been a fan of self-sustainment and found that gardening served as a much-needed reliever of stress and a way for me to take my mind off what was going on.

I spent my free time working with a half dozen tomato, pepper and vegetable plants, along with an assortment of herbs and spices between classes in my backyard in California. Here, I was turning a few hundred meters into a full acre of garden, and was completely in my element.

I had been smart enough to start my own little seed vault back home from making friends with other gardeners and canners, had accrued a respectful assortment of seeds to put to use.

My ex argued tirelessly about the various mason jars scattered throughout our garage with names like "heirloom tomato," "Japanese eggplant" and "poblano peppers," but now they would be our sustenance rather than an annoyance, and I was glad that I had the foresight to keep on with my collection.

The cold storage was the first project finished for the day, and when they were hooked up, the guys tasked with that job came to help us. When we finished sowing all of the seeds, the group made our way to the gun range together to see how our new additions were coming, and to get a few shooting drills in ourselves.

Green Berets love guns more than oxygen, so any chance we could get to shoot or run through shooting drills was like a play-day for us, and we were more than happy to step in and assist the Bravos in their instruction.

The sun started going down as we finished our final iteration of moving and shooting drills with the newbies, which meant it was time for the recon guys to start making their way out on the mission.

Grease, gunpowder and sweat covered us as we made our way from the range back to the team house, and found the guys there already gearing up and getting ready to head out.

As I helped Tony put camouflage on his face, check his radios, cameras, batteries and weapons, each of the others did the same. We called them PCIs, or Pre-Combat Inspections, a way to get a second set of eyes on all-important equipment before a mission to ensure everything was ready.

After the final PCIs, we moved outside for the final radio checks. The guys stood in a circle to make sure they could hear and be heard by all, including the base station situated inside the team house, and going over all foreseeable actions that could occur.

That was a major detail that most people took for granted, but we took very seriously; you never knew what was going to happen on a mission, and while you couldn't plan for everything, it just made life a little easier to have a plan in place in case shit hit the fan, rather than needing to wing it when your life was on the line and things were already going wrong.

If the guys got compromised on any of the objectives, they'd fall back to a rally point and defend until our Quick Reaction Force could find their location and would try to get them out of there with our heavy weapons.

If we got compromised while they were out on the mission, we'd send them a distress call on the radio and fall back to our secondary location, another plot of land we owned about ten miles away, which was smaller and not as well maintained, but a safe place nonetheless.

After the last man got the thumbs-up from the circle that all could hear him speaking into his microphone, it was time to go. We helped the teams load up on the motorcycles and ATVs and watched as they rode out of the gate on their way. If all that The Major told us earlier were true, this would be a huge mission, and one that was important to our cause.

It would give us the opportunity to deal a huge blow to the enemy, free some of our fellow Americans and possibly increase our fighting force even more. I learned about re-education camps used by our enemies in previous wars and spent some time in one myself as all Green Berets do in SERE school, but still couldn't bare to imagine what a real one would look like, especially one full of my people.

I forced myself to stop thinking about those horrible images as I watched the last team ride off into the darkness. We'd know enough about what to expect when they came back with pictures, and I didn't want to scare or anger myself by allowing my imagination to run wild.

We rigged the motorcycles and ATVs for recon missions specifically, so the only lights they used couldn't be seen without night vision goggles. Chris fashioned the carburetors and exhausts so they hardly made any noise, making them the perfect recon vehicles - quiet and quick.

As we heard the dirt kicking up from the last ATV driving down the trail leading out of our back gate, our party turned and started back to join everyone else. It wasn't wise to go on a mission with a full stomach for a multitude of reasons, so the guys heading out that night had eaten some jerky and other small things to tide them over.

But after working on the compound all day the rest of us were famished.

I caught the scents of John's cooking as we made our way from the gate and past the shooting range, past the new cold storage and down into our living area. John and the rest of the newcomers lived in the house above ground, but it was only built as a single-family house, so our underground quarters, which were built to house over a dozen families, had more of the facilities for us all, which included cooking and eating.

John made himself at home almost immediately in the industrial-sized kitchen, and though we built it for usage and efficiency rather than comfort, he organized everything like a proper five-star kitchen within hours of arriving.

As I followed my nose to the kitchen area, I peeked in to see several of the wives helping cut vegetables and prepare plates as John tore through the kitchen like a tornado, adding a dash of spices here and taking a sniff there to ensure everything was just right.

A gaggle of kids bumped into the back of my legs while playing tag up and down the hall, and I heard the intercom system chirp to life.

Chad was on duty in the team house watching our security cameras and listening to the radios, and the tone of his voice over the intercom foreshadowed that he didn't have anything good to tell us.

"Bulldog, Josh, Chris! I need you up here ASAP!"

looked down the hall and watched as the men called began running in the direction of the team house.

"Hurry!" came Chad's voice over the intercom as we moved down the hallway, and we each transitioned from a fast-paced walk to a quick jog.

When I reached the team house and stepped inside, I found Chad talking into the radio and pointing at the video monitors.

We had placed night vision cameras in the woods around our compound, and ground sensors and a FLIR camera that gave us a 360-degree view for a mile around our perimeter, all of which revealed what had Chad so worked up.

"Roger, they're all around us! We're going to need your help," Chad was saying into the radio.

"We've got three recon teams out so we're pretty short-handed right now. I'll have the boss call you back when we have a plan. 022 out."

As Chad put the radio receiver down he walked over to the screens to give us his brief.

"I'm not exactly sure what's going on, but these guys started showing up about ten minutes ago," he said, pointing to groups of soldiers and vehicles massing around our perimeter.

"The sensors started going crazy on all sides as they began closing in. I caught them on the FLIR moving this way and then, all of a sudden, they all just stopped right where they are now."

"How far out are they?" asked Chris.

"They're about half a mile out right now, surrounding us at about 270 degrees. I'm guessing they can't get into this side because of the terrain," he said, pointing to another screen showing the southern part of our perimeter.

"Good," said Josh. "That's how we planned it. That mountain face on our backside would scare even a billy goat and would be suicide for anyone who didn't know their way around back there to try and come in. The scary part is that if they know that, that means they've been watching us."

"Have you been in contact with the other teams?" Bulldog asked Chad.

"I was speaking with The Major when you got here; they know we're in trouble, but didn't get to the part about whether they were sending help or not."

"I'll get on the horn with them, and you guys start getting ready to roll out," said Bulldog as he moved toward the radio.

"Send a runner out to let the guys on the wire know what's happening! No radio communication between us with the handhelds - we don't want them listening and knowing that we have an escape route or that we were alerted they're here."

Buckeye gave a thumbs up us as he started moving towards the guard posts, and Josh added another directive.

"Get to your families," he pointed at all of us.

"They'll just add to the confusion, so get them in the trucks first and then start getting our gear. JLo, go start the engines. Griz, get the go bags ready and hook the trailers up to the vehicles. We don't know how much time we have till they hit us, but it can't be long."

Just as I started to make my way outside to get my family, a ball of light and wave of heat knocked me off of my feet and onto the ground, and as my head smacked the hard clay, I heard the explosion.

Having been on both the giving and receiving ends of several IEDs [Improvised Explosive Devices] in my time, I knew this was much larger, and didn't come from the ground.

"What was that?" Klint yelled as he picked me up.

"That came from the air," answered Ray. "Time to get the hell out of here!"

As the men came out of the team room, everyone scattered in their various directions. Ray had been running to the living quarters when the explosion hit, and as soon as he picked himself up off the ground made a beeline back for the team house.

He was only inside for a few seconds when I saw the entire forest surrounding our compound light up in an eruption like the gates of hell had been opened.

Being a huge fan of demolitions and having a father who served as a Green Beret in Vietnam, Ray had been working on his own pet project from the first day we built this compound - and it had just saved our lives.

A tactic begun by our Vietnam era Brothers but forgotten during our incursions in the deserts of the Middle East, foo gas was a last-ditch effort used in the jungle A-camps inhabited by Special Forces ODAs who were being overrun by the enemy.

Foo gas is a line of oil drums filled with gas, explosives, and homemade napalm, so once Ray hit the red initiator buttons lining one of our walls in the team house, the fires and explosions that erupted from the dozens of foo gas canisters he hid outside of our perimeter set the trees - and our enemy - ablaze.

Even at a half-mile away, my senses were overcome by enemy screams with the telltale stench of napalm and cooking meat as it burned at their flesh. Hastily turning my attention back to my family, I began running to our living quarters as fast as my legs would carry me.

I ran past the house above ground, now engulfed in flames from the direct hit of whatever it was that caused the explosion. I wasn't entirely sure if it was a bomb or artillery shell, but as I made my way toward the living quarters, people began to emerge and run in the direction of the house.

"Get to the trucks, get to the trucks!" I began to yell as the running bodies drew closer and closer, and when they became close enough for me to see their faces, I understood why they weren't paying any attention to me.

They were the newcomers, those who had been living in that house - and escaping was not one of the things at the top of their minds.

Leaping down the entire staircase in one jump, I ran into Sarah, holding my daughter in her arms and on her way towards the exit.

"Get the kids and get to the trucks. Don't worry about any of your stuff, just get in the truck and get it started up," I told her as I tried to pull away. Grabbing on to my shirt, she showed a look of absolute terror in her eyes.

"I don't know where Robert is! Avery was sleeping in the room, but Robert was playing with the other kids and I don't know where they are!"

"Just find him," I told her. "I'll take care of everything else. Just find him and get to the truck now! We don't have much time!"

Turning and trying to remember everything I needed to grab, I sprinted towards my room. I still had a few empty bags that I could use, and I was going to need to bring every bit of medicine and medical gear possible.

As I hurried back out of the room and towards the clinic, I nearly ran over my son Robert, terrified and crying.

"Daddy, what's going on?" he asked me between tears and jumped into my arms.

The explosion and subsequent chaos was too much for his little four-year-old mind to take, but I didn't have the time to explain it to him.

"Sarah!" I yelled down the hall.

"Sarah!" I repeated as loudly as I could.

When I saw her poke her head out of one of the common rooms, I pointed Robert in her direction.

"Go to miss Sarah, buddy, and I'll meet you guys at the truck."

As soon as I pointed him in her direction and let go, he ran towards her as fast as he could.

Knowing that they were together now, it was time for me to grab everything I could. We had some supplies at our fallback location but nothing near what was at our primary, so we needed everything we could find.

The second my bags were filled with every IV and antibiotic I could carry, I ran out of the clinic and started sprinting to the stairs. I had one more stop before I was ready to go, and I needed to get there as quickly as possible.

The sound of the vehicles' engines running echoed in the underground garage as I ran up the stairs and into the night air.

When I dropped my bags to run to the greenhouse, the heavy guns at our guard positions opened up. I guessed the foo gas slowed the enemy down but hadn't quite stopped them.

Sprinting across the open courtyard and to the greenhouse, I prayed that we would make it out of there safely. The rounds from enemy small arms fire began to whiz past me, indicating they were getting close enough for effective fire and that I was running out of time.

Reaching the greenhouse, I swung the door open and grabbed the airtight tough box that housed what was perhaps one of our most precious commodities now: the seeds.

As I began to run back across the courtyard with the seeds in my arms, several people were sitting on their knees in front of the house.

I wasn't quite sure what they were doing at first, sitting out in the open as enemy rounds whizzed all around us, but it became obvious as I ran closer.

The women were wailing and as their mournful cries grew louder, the stark reality hit me. While the adults were downstairs getting ready for dinner, the children had been napping soundly in their beds upstairs - which was nothing more than a burning crater now.

As I made my way to grab and drag the adults to the vehicles, another explosion knocked me to the ground. Jumping back up, I found another wall of fire just outside of our perimeter this time, meaning the enemy was within a hundred meters of our fence line.

This time, I not only heard the screams of men as the skin melted off their bodies, but I could see their fiery outlines too, running and looking for anything to put out the flames and stop the pain. That was the thing with foo gas and napalm - once you're hit, nothing short of death would end your suffering.

I grabbed the first mourning and wailing person that I came to - Jacob's wife - and began to drag her back towards the vehicles. She kicked and screamed the entire way, and I ended up having to throw her over my shoulder and fireman's-carry her to the garage.

By the time I had her seated in the back of the Bradley, she was sobbing uncontrollably, but there was no time to stop and comfort her. I saw Sarah and the kids in our Land Rover Defender with her behind the wheel, and she caught my gaze as I nodded and made my way back up top.

I could see several of the guys pulling in the other adults who had been weeping and wailing in front of the burning remains of the house, so I ran back to grab my bags of medical gear.

As I bent over to pick them up, a flurry of rounds exploded into the wooden wall just above my head, and in a quick fit of rage, I brought my rifle around and expended an entire magazine of rounds through the chain-link fence surrounding our compound as I walked forward.

When I heard the *click* signifying my magazine was empty, I took a knee, switched the safety off the M203 grenade launcher affixed to the bottom of my rifle, angled it up around 75 degrees and let one fly.

As soon as I replaced the round in my M203, I remembered my purpose, and ran back to the medical bags. They were over my shoulder in seconds, and as I moved toward the garage I saw the first of the vehicles come up the steep drive and turn in the direction of our escape route.

I was relieved when the Defender appeared in the driveway with Sarah in the driver's seat. It followed the convoy to the exit. I knew would be right behind her in the Bradley with the heavy guns, but still felt a twinge of panic when I saw the car seats in the passenger row behind her occupied by my children.

I could hear that someone had already started the Bradley as I ran down the driveway into the garage.

As I opened the back hatch to the passenger compartment, I found that we were full, but not quite as full as we had been the last time I took it out on a mission. Dropping the bags in a few empty seats I jumped into the driver's seat, slammed it into gear and began to back out.

Ray was still in the team house so I pulled up outside the front door as soon as I was above ground, and just as I saw his devilishly-grinning face appear in the doorway and point to the front gate, there was another blinding explosion that erupted, even closer to our perimeter this time.

"Somehow they still haven't learned that I really like to make things go boom. Just wait till they get in here and find my last surprise!" he yelled as he jumped into the gunner's nest and I floored it.

We were a few minutes behind the rest of the convoy, and when I turned the Bradley as hard as I could in the middle of the compound, I heard Ray turn the turret to our rear and open up with the 25mm cannon. After a few seconds, I heard him come over the radio.

"Stop stop stop, Rob, stop!" he yelled.

Not knowing what was going on, I slammed on the brakes and the Bradley's wheels halted in their tracks.

"Ten seconds!" Ray yelled.

I looked up to see him aiming the TOW missiles.

"We got mechanized, but not for long!"

Looking at my screen I saw there were several armored vehicles running down our fencing in various sections around the front gate, and as soon as the first one broke through, I heard a *whoosh* and felt the Bradley rock backwards as Ray launched the first missile. He let the second one fly as soon as the first exploded on its target.

"Ok, Rob, go go go go go!" he yelled down at me.

I slammed on the gas again and we were off, following in the footsteps of the rest of our convoy along the escape route. We couldn't move very fast along our route, but because of the way it had been constructed there was no way the enemy would find it this quickly. And with the explosives lining the entrance to the underground portion which led out of our compound, Ray would have a nice little surprise for anyone who was sly enough to find it.

The tunnel was quite a testament to our engineers, actually, and just went to show that give an 18C enough explosives and he can do just about anything.

Anything for us was tunneling an underground passageway big enough for a tank underneath the mountain flanking our compound. Surprisingly enough, they didn't lose a single finger in the process.

By the time we arrived at the fallback location, the rest of the convoy had already dismounted and the men had taken up a defensive posture as the women moved the gear and supplies into the living facilities. It definitely wouldn't be as comfortable here as the last compound, but at least we were alive, and that was all we could ask for.

Josh made his way over to the Bradley before I had a chance to shut it down and gave us our commands.

"Rob, you and Ray take up a defensive position on the north side of the compound. If they knew about the last place, there's a chance they'll know about this one, so we've got to stay on our guard. If anybody goes into that tunnel on the other side, blow it."

"Roger," smiled Ray as he held up his remote initiator for the explosives-laden tunnel.

"Did we get the radios and all the sensitive equipment out of there in time?" I asked.

"Yeah, we knew that was probably going to happen at some point, so it didn't take much to have everything packed up and out of there."

"Did we get word to the guys outside the wire that we were leaving?"

"Yeah, Chad said he got a hold of Jason and Matty, but couldn't raise Tattoo or Corey. Still no word from them, but we raised the IR chem lights on the flagpole to let them know what was up in case they don't get our message on the radio."

"Did everybody make it out?" I knew the answer, but needed some confirmation.

"Not quite. The house was full of kids when it got hit, but thankfully some of them were running around playing tag with us underground. The ones that were sleeping in the house though...not a single one made it out. It looks like Jacob was up there too, so tonight was a pretty heavy loss."

"So what do we do now?" I asked.

"For now," Josh paused, looking up at the stars, "for now you watch that north fence until someone comes to relieve you. Beyond that, we'll have to figure out tomorrow."

"Roger that," I answered and watched Josh as he walked off into the darkness.

CHAPTER 9

BLOOD LUST

It was "stand-to" or first light when we got the call from the first recon team coming in.

As they say in the Ranger Handbook, "*Dawn is when the French and Indians attack*." So when the sun rises, any infantryman or Special Operations soldier is awake, in their foxhole and ready for anything.

"Eagles coming in," Tony's voice called over the radio.

"Come on in, Eagles" replied Chad from the team room.

I watched from my post high up on the fence line as the tall and lean outline of Jason rode through the front gate on the motorcycle, and Tony's python-sized forearms gripping the ATV handles followed quickly after.

I wanted to run down and press them for every piece of intel they got, ask if they saw any of the troops headed our way, and most importantly, if they had seen or heard from Tattoo and Corey.

But my place was at my post, standing guard until we could get the FLIR system up to give us a good view of our surroundings. This was our fallback, and thankfully we had this, but if the enemy knew about this location and blew us out here, we didn't have anywhere else to go.

I turned my attention back to the forest and mountains surrounding us, and listened as the guys shut their vehicles down in front of the team house. I could even hear Tony loudly exclaim a few choice expletives as he dismounted the ATV to head inside and spill every piece of information he gleaned the night before.

Stand-to was an eerie time of the day for me, and had been since the first time I had ever taken part in one during our first field exercise in Infantry basic training. They say sound travels louder and farther in the dark, but I'd argue that your imagination travels further during stand-to.

I'm not sure if it's because your eyes are adjusting from the darkness of night back to the newfound light of day, if it's the fact that in the field you never eat enough, if your sleep-deprived brain is creating shadows and ghosts in lieu of sleep and dreams, or if it's because you're expecting the enemy to come at any given second, but with every furtive glance and shift of my eyes, I saw an advance coming for us.

As the dawn of the morning gave way to full light, we heard the second call - from Matty this time.

"Eagles coming in, two minutes out."

"Come on in, Eagles," came the reply again from Chad.

I watched Matty coming through the gates on his motorcycle, followed closely by Adam on the ATV.
This meant everyone stood accounted for, save for Tattoo and Corey.

As I watched Matty and Adam begin to dismount, the silhouette of Josh against the cold new light of the morning began to make its way towards Ray. After a few moments of furtive conversation, I saw Josh make his way back to the team house and heard Ray come over the radio.

"Detonation in thirty seconds."

The foo gas had done its primary job of giving us enough time to make a clean escape from the compound, but now it was time to fulfill its secondary task.

As there was no way to be 100% sure that we were able to grab every piece of confidential information, map, personal material or anything that would give away our identities, new locations, radio frequencies and the like, the only thing left to do was to destroy everything.

As I viewed Ray's profile, about a hundred meters away from me and huddled in the dark, I hoped that every enemy soldier remained on our compound, perhaps thinking they were going to make it home with one of John's nice bottles of booze, or enjoying the meal he had been cooking up.

Ray held up the last remote initiator, and as he began counting down from ten, my mind went to some very dark places. Hate may keep you warm in the cold dawn of day, but I could tell mine was starting to get to dangerous levels.

As Ray finally reached two on his countdown, I transitioned my gaze to the direction of our old compound. We traveled quite a distance underground and through a mountain tunnel, so there was no realistic chance I'd see the explosion, but I had to try anyway.

While the foo gas around our perimeter was a pretty healthy dose and enough to take out hundreds of enemy troops, the demolitions that Ray hid around our compound was enough to destroy the place several times over.

Even from our new location ten miles away and on the other side of a mountain, I felt the ground shake below me as Ray depressed the initiator. I silently hoped that the explosion sent our enemies to the darkest parts of hell imaginable, but not before a long and painful death.

It was another hour of scanning the horizon for any enemy movement before Josh came back out to the line, and walked to each man to disseminate the information of what was going on and what was going to happen.

They had been in contact with The Major and his team, who were currently en route to our new location. His group hadn't been able to come to our defense while the compound was under attack, and that was probably for good reason. A dozen guys was no match for tanks and artillery, even with the element of surprise.

Josh explained that our priority now was getting Tattoo and Corey back, and The Major said that he knew where they were.

The Standard Operating Procedure [SOP] in other wars was to get enemy who had high-level information off the battlefield as quickly as possible, which meant we didn't have long to get our boys back.

The Russians, for example, would use several levels of interrogations. This meant Tattoo and Corey were most likely going through a field interrogation at the moment somewhere close by, which was the first level.

These were typically the most violent and painful interrogations, led by soldiers who didn't know much about the psychology of a real interrogation or how to get information.

Their job was mainly to cause pain and terror.

After the field interrogation, they would be moved to a higher-level interrogator in-country. This level would be a little more skilled and may use fear, sleep deprivation or other tactics in place of sheer pain and violence, and proved to be more effective.

But the clock that we were running against was the last level of interrogation, that which had been widely used in every major war.

This entailed sending the Prisoner of War [POW] back to the enemy's home country, where they would be imprisoned and interrogated for possibly years to come.

This level would be enacted by high-level intelligence agents whose sole purpose in life was to glean information from people without them even knowing they were giving anything away.

If Tattoo and Corey got to this level, not only would we need to worry about the enemy knowing our names, backgrounds, where our fallback position was and future battle plans, but there would be no chance to get our friends back alive.

Josh explained we had two missions that needed to be pursued immediately.

First and foremost, go get our Brothers. Second, we had to go back to our primary compound to search for anything salvageable and see to it nothing was left which could give away our new location.

As he finished with me and began moving further down the line, I mentally prepared myself for a long next few days. After leaving Special Forces, everyone I met loved to ask me what made a Green Beret, what made us tick, and how someone became one.

The joking answer was that you had to be a little insane, but there was truth hidden within the joke.

The thing that separates a Green Beret from other soldiers isn't that we're fearless robots that can go for days and days without recharge. In reality, we're just as scared as everyone else to run face-first into a wave of bullets or explosions.

But at the end of the day, the thing that truly separates a Green Beret is an absolute mastery of the basics, and having those basics so strongly enforced into our muscle memory that we could enact them flawlessly no matter how tired, hungry, stressed out or absolutely terrified we were.

Special Forces missions could last hours or days without food or sleep and always moving forward. But if it was something as important as getting our Brothers back, not a single one of us would hesitate for a second.

About an hour after my conversation with Josh, I heard footsteps behind me and turned to view a giant of a man in a multi-cam uniform making his way towards me. As soon as he got to my position he lay on the ground beside me with his rifle pointed forward.

"You, Rob?" he asked me in a hushed but deep and husky voice.

"I am. Who the hell are you?" I asked in reply.

"I'm Dave," he answered from behind his dark Oakleys.

"I think you met our leader, The Major. We just got here and heard you guys didn't get a lot of rest last night so I'm giving you a break. I think we're heading out as soon as the sun goes down, so you should go back and get some sleep. I've got your position here."

I glanced up and over Dave's head to find another figure next to Ray, probably explaining the same thing. Looking back at Dave I realized just how tired I was and figured a little nap couldn't hurt, so I began to get up and make my way back to the team house.

Ray walked in just a few steps behind me and we found the team house was a flurry of activity. Bulldog, Josh and The Major were hunched over a map, talking and drawing out battle plans when we entered the room, and the pictures from our recon guys had already been plastered on the walls.

"Morning, boys!" The Major exclaimed to us as we made our way in. I could still see the black battle-axe hanging from his belt and chuckled.

"The Major and his guys are here to help us hit the POW camp tonight," Bulldog explained before we even asked.

"The chances of Corey and Tattoo being held there for the time being are pretty high. The clock is ticking on how long they'll be there before being flown out of the country, so we need to hit them tonight."

Josh walked to the pictures on the board and added his piece.

"No new prisoners were brought in to either of the other camps last night while our guys were watching, so the one Tattoo and Corey were on is the one we're hitting tonight. We're rolling out as soon as the sun goes down, so you guys get some rest. Someone will come wake you up when it's time to go."

I nodded in my fog-filled haziness and sleepy state; I didn't have anything to say that would help, and was too tired to come up with any good questions, so I turned and followed Ray out of the team house and back to our new living quarters.

It felt like I just laid my head on the pillow when I woke to Robert nudging my shoulder and looking at me.

"What time is it?" I asked. "Didn't I just lay down?"

"You've been asleep for the entire day, daddy. It's four o'clock and Uncle Chris told me to come and wake you up."

I tossed my feet over the side of the bed and held my head in my hands while I tried to wake up. Robert began rubbing my sore and aching back as I bent over to put on my socks and boots.

"Where are you going tonight, daddy?" he questioned.

"To get our guys back," I answered.

He was too young to understand anything more than that. As I tightened and tied the laces on my boots, he gave me a pat on the back. I stood up and turned around to give him a kiss, picked him up in my arms and carried him to play with the rest of the kids before making my way back up to the team house.

Everything at our new location was a bit smaller, and with twice the men here now it felt pretty crowded when I walked in. Some guys were topping off their magazines with ammo, Ray and Chris were putting duct tape over the pins of grenades so they wouldn't be pulled accidentally, and Josh, Bulldog and The Major were at the front of the room prepared to brief.

As soon as they saw everyone gathered in the room, Josh called out for us to take a seat and quiet down.

When the last of us took seats in chairs, on the floor or rested our backs against the wall, Bulldog pointed at a series of pictures situated around the red outline indicating our target on the map.

"Men, let me direct your attention to Objective Papa Charlie One, more commonly known as Prison Camp one. Out of the three prison camps in the Denver area, this is by far the largest and most logistically supported, which is good and bad."

The Major stepped in to add his piece.

"As Bulldog said, this is good because we are about 90% sure this is where Corey and Tattoo are being held until the enemy can get flight capabilities back and get them out of country. It's bad because, well, they've got a lot of men guarding this place, so we'll have to be on our A-game tonight."

"This place has a relatively small perimeter," Josh added, "and as you can see from the pictures, the middle of the camp is comprised of nothing but cages, like cattle cages. This is where the majority of the people they've been rounding up are being held."

He looked around the room to make sure we understood what he was saying.

"That means we need to be on target with every round boys. The people in here are packed pretty tightly, shoulder-to-shoulder in some areas, meaning one stray bullet or M203 round could cause a lot of civilian damage. Make sure everyone is on target and carefully aimed.

We're here to save Americans - not have them be collateral damage."

The Major stepped in again.

"And as you can see, the layout will make that pretty difficult. As it's a relatively small compound, anybody firing has the potential to hit those cages in the middle. This is a textbook prison camp complete with guard towers on all sides, triple strand concertina wire along the perimeter and flood lights illuminating the surrounding areas."

"So what's the plan?" asked Jason from the corner.

"It's going to take each of us being on time and on target, but we think we can get away with it," answered Josh.

"These buildings here are obviously the barracks," he said, pointing to a row of buildings on one side of the compound, marked with a red X.

"And these," he said pointing to buildings on the other side, "are the headquarters and office buildings, indicated by the letters HQ."

"They have armed guards in the towers at all times, guards patrolling the fence line, and guards patrolling the cages. We don't have time to tunnel under them, we don't have the resources for a typical raid, so this is going to need to be a little unconventional."

Josh looked around the room to make sure we were all tracking.

"How unconventional?" asked Tony with his arms folded on his chest.

"Since we need to get in there ASAP, we're going to use the element of surprise and violence of action to pull this one off," answered Bulldog.

"We're lucky that they don't have any armor on this compound, and there is no real barricade at the front entrance. It's nothing more than some concertina wire and a chain link fence, and since we have the Bradley--"

"Wait a minute, are you saying what I think you're saying?" interrupted Adam.

"Yup" answered Josh.

"We're ramming the front gate."

There were audible grumbles and murmurs around the room, to which The Major stepped up to quiet them down.

"Is there anyone in this room who hasn't heard of the Son Tay raid?" he asked.

That seemed to quiet everyone down, so he continued.

"A few dozen Green Berets in Vietnam took down a compound larger than this under pretty similar circumstances."

"Yeah, but they had a helicopter," added Griz.

"And the POWs they went to save weren't even there!" bellowed Ray.

"AT EASE!" Chris yelled from the back of the room with his thunderous voice.

"Why don't all of you keep your damn comments to yourself and hear these guys out. Two of our troops are sitting in that camp being beaten to death as we speak, and unless we get in there tonight, we'll never see them again. So shut up and listen, and if you don't want to take part in this mission, you have every right to opt out - just make sure the door doesn't hit you on the ass on your way out."

With the walls still echoing from Chris' commands, Bulldog started in again.

"Thanks, Chris. Like I was saying, any good raid starts with a diversion."

After Bulldog finished his piece we all felt a little more at ease. Unconventional Warfare was our bread and butter, and this mission would be a textbook example of what exactly that meant.

If this had been a typical mission in Iraq or Afghanistan we would never have gone in with this little support, but this was anything except a typical mission, and time was of the essence.

Each of us knew exactly what would happen to our Brothers, Tattoo and Corey, if we didn't get to them before they were sent out of country, and none of us wanted to explain that to their families.

As this was such a time-sensitive target, there was no time to rest or pose an academic debate about strategy. We were going to hit them hard, hit them fast, get our Brothers back and drop the hammer on the enemy's offensive.

I spent the remainder of the day working on the trucks and stashing medical gear in every nook and cranny I found. We had to anticipate dealing with casualties from our men on this mission as well as the possibility of civilian casualties, not to mention those I may need to attend to from the savage beatings enacted by their captors in the camp.

When I finished putting every piece of gauze bandage, tourniquet, IV and pressure dressing I could spare in the trucks, I walked over to admire the Charlies doing their thing.

As I watched them building the largest bomb I had ever seen in a five-ton truck loaded with nothing but explosives in the back, I couldn't help but think how well this would fit into a cheesy military television show.

But in all seriousness, it had worked before, and it was the only way we could plausibly get in there. There weren't enough snipers to take out all of the guard towers, we couldn't risk an errant mortar hitting the civilians caged in the middle of the compound, and we didn't have the luxury of tanks, aside from our one Bradley.

As the sun started to set and the Charlies put the finishing touches on our five-ton IED, we exchanged a few nervous jokes while marveling at their creation. For all of the technology we had at our disposal, for all of the fancy weapons and tools we used in the past, the key to what was possibly the most important mission in any of

our careers was all dependent on something as cliché as a truck full
of explosives, driven by a brick on the accelerator and a
rope tied to the steering wheel.

But it was all we had, and it was just silly enough to work.

Dinner was both lighter and quieter than any I ever
remembered around this crowd. Tattoo and Corey's wives sat in the
center of everyone, and it helped us to remember just how
important it was that this mission be a success.

If we failed our mission, not only would we lose our Brothers,
but we'd most likely lose more of our already outmanned fighting
force. We just couldn't risk that, not now.

Bulldog and The Major's watches both beeped at the same time,
letting everyone know it was time to go. The single men started to
get up and make their way towards the team houses, as those with
families took a moment to hug, kiss and promise their loved ones
that they would be home before they woke up.

Robert and Avery could sense that this wasn't a time for
questions, and they both gave me the strongest hugs they had to
date as I knelt down and held them in my arms.

"You take care of your sister while I'm gone, ok, buddy?" I said
to Robert.

"When are you coming home, daddy?"

"I should be home before you wake up."

"What if you don't come home?"

"Daddy always comes home to you, buddy. I promise I'll be
home, I just can't promise when."

"Where are you going, daddy?"

"Daddy's got to go to work, buddy."

"Back at the hospital?"

"No," I answered as I kissed his forehead. "No, daddy has to go
get his friends back. That's daddy's job now. I love you both very
much. I'll be back soon. Watch over your sister until I get back."
"Ok, daddy, I wuv you too," he replied with an even tighter hug.

I knew that if I hesitated any longer it would be next to
impossible for me to leave, so I forced myself to stand up, turn
around and walk as fast as I could to the trucks without looking back.

The trucks were already running with the other guys gathered in the typical pre-mission circle in front of them, checking their communications and going over the plan.

As soon as I responded over the radio and was met with the thumbs up of everyone in the circle indicating they could hear me, Josh went over the plan one more time to ensure we were all on the same page.

As he finished and was met with nods all around that the group was ready, he gave the signal to get in the trucks and start moving.

The sniper element was rolling out first on motorcycles to make less noise, as the rest of the trucks would split into two elements: our team in front, the explosive-laden five-ton in the middle of the convoy and The Major's team in the rear.

The ride to the camp was much shorter than I imagined, or maybe the time just went by quickly as all I could think about were our actions on the objective, and just how fast and surgically this whole thing would have to go down.

We didn't know just how advanced the enemy's technology was, so when we passed our rally point in the trucks, The Major's team broke off in another direction without a word.

We couldn't risk our radio transmissions being picked up, so everything from that point forward would have to be non-verbal communication.

Using nothing more than hand and arm signals between the gunners in their turrets, our convoy stopped to prepare for the initiation. Our snipers had ridden far ahead of us on their motorcycles, and were hopefully already perched high in their locations, away from sight and with the tower guards in their sights.

If they missed their shots and the guards had enough time to sound the alarm at the truck barreling towards the front gate, the mission would be a failure.

As it would be if we couldn't get through the front gate before enemy reinforcements arrived with RPGs and heavy machine guns, or if we couldn't get our boots on the ground to start looking for and finding Tattoo and Corey quickly. It all boiled down to those initial shots.

The enemy had been smart enough to clear several hundred meters of trees on all sides of the POW camp, so we lined up our trucks in the tree line. The five-ton was put on line to the front gate with me behind it in the Bradley, the HUMVEE behind me and another soft skin truck behind that. Now it was just time to wait for the go signal.

As I waited behind the wheel, all I could do was stare at my watch. The snipers were supposed to take the guards out at 0200 hours exactly, and the second the guards went down we'd set the five-ton on its fateful route.

My task was to drive the Bradley as close behind the five-ton as possible, which had me a little nervous. To make this work I would need to follow the explosion right into the compound, make an entrance for the rest of the team and be the first one on the objective.

The seconds climbed closer and closer from 0159 and up, and as I whispered to Ray that we only had 30 seconds left, he raised his binoculars to observe the towers closest to us.

He counted down from ten seconds, and I watched Bulldog stand next to the five-ton with his own set of binoculars. As soon as Ray's count reached its end, he simultaneously exclaimed,

"Bingo!" as Bulldog turned to Buckeye and directed him to set the truck on its course.

Thankfully, the brick on the five-ton's accelerator had it moving pretty fast, because the 200 meters of completely open terrain I needed to drive between the wood line and front gate seemed to stretch on forever.

My nervousness was quickly replaced with adrenaline as the front gate exploded in a glorious fireball. I was close enough to feel the heat of the shockwave when the explosive-laden truck reached its target, and the ensuing explosion was strong enough to push me back in my seat.

No time to marvel at the force and destruction, I slammed on the gas and tore through the front gate, still a raging wall of fire and smoke, ramming the burning hull of what was left of the five-ton out of my way as I drove into the middle of the compound.

Ray opened up with the 20mm cannon the moment we were in the compound, and immediately saw that we caught the enemy with their pants down.

I don't know if they were so brazen that they just didn't expect us to attack them, mistakenly thought they killed us when they raided our compound, or were just too lazy to be on-guard. The few soldiers who were awake around the compound were quickly neutralized by Ray, who then turned his attention to vaporizing the barracks into nothing more than smoke and dust.

As I watched Ray demolish the entire barracks complex, the other two trucks sped past us and made their way straight towards the enemy headquarters building.

The assault team was already jumping out of the trucks before they came to a halt, and in the blink of an eye, they stacked in formation outside of the front door, threw a few concussion grenades inside and were in as the smoke was still clearing.

Chris emerged just moments later, carrying a bleeding and screaming officer with him. It only took a few punches from the metal plated knuckles on his glove for the officer to pull something out of his pocket and hand it over to Chris, which was met with a smile and a final blow to the face.

He looked at the key card the officer surrendered over for a second, back at us in the trucks and returned into the headquarters building.

The rest of the team emerged within minutes, carrying Tattoo and Corey with them, bruised and beaten, and placed them in the backs of the trucks. As soon as the guys were situated, they drove to meet us.

"Rob, we're going to need you on this one! We've got to go clear those cages and get any Americans we find out of here."

"Roger that, Josh," I replied.

"You and Griz take the first row, Ray will stay here and lock down the area. We don't have long until their reinforcements show up, so let's get a move on."

As Josh turned to give his orders to the other truck, I dismounted, linked up with Griz and started towards the first set of cages. As we made our way down the rows, opening the cages with the key Chris gave to Griz, I noticed something that stopped me in my tracks.

"Griz, get over here!" I yelled to Griz who was a few cages behind me.

He caught up to me in a matter of seconds.

"What's up, Rob?" he gasped.

"You recognize those guys?" I asked, pointing to the men interspersed with women and children in the next cage.

"Holy shit," he replied, immediately recognizing the men's faces from their countless hours on television.

"What do we do?" he asked.

"I got this, just wanted to make sure I wasn't seeing things." As Griz went back to opening the cages on his side, I stepped in front of the next gate.

"Okay, women and children to the left, men to the right!" I yelled.

An older, overweight man in a torn and tattered suit stepped defiantly towards the fence and began yelling.

"We're not leaving our families."

"I'm not asking you to leave your families," I replied.

"Well then what are you doing separating us?" he screamed as close as he could get to my face.

"I'm asking your families to leave you."

"I think you're mistaken there, son. Don't you know who I am?" he spat like a madman.

"I know exactly who you are, Senator. You're one of the reasons this is all happening. You supported disarming the people. You supported decimating the military. You supported running our country as far into the ground as possible for your own gain, raping and pillaging our land and getting every penny you could. I know exactly who you are, which is why you and every other politician in here is staying put."

A new voice, one which I recognized from long, blustery windbag speeches on the House floor, spoke up from the back.

"Well if you're not taking all of us, you're not taking any of us!"

Looking around the cage I found various pig-faced men, used to getting their way standing with their arms crossed looking stern-faced at me.

"Have it your way," I replied back into the cage as I moved down the line towards the next one.

"Wait!" a few female voices rang out.

I turned to see women and children huddling around the gate of the political prisoner's cage, with several men interspersed with them.

"You," I said, pointing at a lifelong politician that I recognized from her destruction of California.

"You get over there with the rest of the scum."

"I don't think you understand who I am, young man. If anyone is leaving here, it's going to
be--"

She stopped in her tracks as I pulled out my 1911 pistol and pointed it directly at her forehead.

"Move," I said, staring her dead in the eyes, to which she slowly shuffled in with the other scum taking up the side of the cage farthest from the gate.

As soon as she was segregated, I pressed the electronic key against the door and it swung open.

"Trucks are at the end of this corridor," I said, pointing in the direction we had come from.

As I turned my attention back to the cage, I saw several of the politicians running straight for the gate, knocking every woman and child out of the way to try and save their own necks.

I raised my 1911 as I approved what I was about to do in my mind. My barrel was almost pointed directly at the first ones oncoming face when I heard the shots.

Two explosions came in quick succession, and as I saw the rounds tear through the back of the first politicians head and heard the screams of women behind him now sprayed in his brain matter, I looked over at Griz, standing with his pistol still at full-length.

"Damn, that felt good!" he said with a smile. "I can't tell you how many times I've watched these scumbags running their sucks on the news and thought about this. Let's finish off the rest and do the world a favor."

As he took a step forward to do just that, I stopped him with a hand on his shoulder.

"What's about to be done to these guys is worse than anything we could ever dream up.

Remember, they didn't only wreck our country, but the entire world economy along with it. Let's get the innocents out of here. We're not the only people in line with a grudge against them."

Griz kept his pistol trained on the group of men, and as the last of the women and children exited the cage, I closed and locked the door.

"You can't really be serious!" another politician yelled out with a southern accent.

I paused briefly to make sure this was what I wanted to do.

"Everyone has to pay for their sins at some point. Karma's a motherfucker," I replied as I turned, walked to the next cage, swung the gate open and pointed the newly freed to their ride home.

CHAPTER 10

SEPARATE WAYS

It was the sound of the chainsaw and subsequent screams that finally did me in.

The surgical saw was the most difficult thing for me to get used to during my orthopedic surgery internship, especially with the smell it created while sawing live human bone.

But the fact that the surgical saw had been replaced with a dull and rusty chainsaw used to cut wood, and the "patients" were enemy soldiers we had taken prisoner and brought back from the mission with us (fully awake and screaming) just didn't sit well with me.

The mission had gone off without a hitch, and since our base was much closer than The Major's, the decision was made to come back to ours for the after-action review.

Not only had we come back from the POW camp with Corey and Tattoo, along with dozens of former captives and as much equipment and weaponry as we could carry, but some of the guys took it upon themselves to take a few prisoners of their own.

We all knew what an interrogation consisted of, and I had partaken in more than a few during our combat deployments together, sometimes taking turns being the good guy, the one who offers the food, drinks, and friendly ear for bad guys to spill their secrets to.

And sometimes I played the bad guy too, and quite honestly took a little pleasure in the unadulterated pain I could inflict with a scalpel, vice grip and a pair of pliers. But this was a little much, even for my taste.

The moment our review was over, rather than getting to our priorities of work, a group of guys made their way to the cramped, dark underground room where we housed the prisoners.

It started innocently enough. As per standard operating procedure, a few of us stayed put outside of the room, taking copious notes on everything the prisoners said while the two men inside grilled them, taking turns asking questions and pummeling them with their fists.

The point of taking copious notes is to find when the prisoner slips up, so we would rotate the two men inside every fifteen minutes, and the new group replacing them would ask the same exact questions.

Any time we were given a change of story or any significant variation from the story we had been hearing, we knew we found something to focus on.

The interrogation took a turn for the worse when The Major went in with one of his men. I could tell the ante was immediately upped by the tone he started with; in SERE we would call it "the hard room," which is EXACTLY what it sounds like.

Stepping away from protocol, the Major and his partner first started with the pain part of their interrogation, not even asking questions but each choosing to get a few licks in on the first prisoner.

Without ever asking any questions, they moved from the first room into the second room to visit the other prisoner. And after a few smashed fingers via a hammer they started into the third room.

It was only then that Dave, the first of The Major's men whom I met, filled me in. Their team had taken some serious losses, both civilian and military.

Not only had their team sergeant been killed in the first few days of fighting, but apparently The Major's best friend was killed in the initial invasion, and his brother had been killed during one of their raids.

Intense yelling began erupting from The Major in the third room, followed by a loud thud and the screams of agony that didn't come from just getting punched. As The Major walked out of the room shadowed by his partner, he carried the battle-axe in his right hand, lightly gripping the handle as the blade drug along the ground behind him leaving a thick and wet pool of dark, red blood.

"You should probably get in there, Doc. I think that guy needs some help," he said, more to the wall than to me, as he walked right back into the first room.

His partner followed close behind hiding something behind his back, and it was only when he got to the first door that we saw what it was - the prisoners amputated and bleeding hand - which he threw on the table in front of the first prisoner as The Major started to ask him questions in a low but violent tone.

I could tell that this was going to get out of hand rather quickly, but as I protested to Tony, he pointed to the third room.

"Just get in there and stop that guy from bleeding out, Doc. He can't help us if he's dead."

Knowing that I wasn't going to get much further with any arguing, I went in to find the prisoner unconscious, still chained to his table face-down in a pool of blood with the stump of his forearm in front of him.

Not wanting to waste antibiotics on someone who most likely wouldn't survive the night anyway, I slapped a pressure dressing on the stump and left the room.

I walked out and was met by the same pain-induced screams coming from the first room. I watched as The Major moved into the second room, followed by his partner, this time carrying two amputated and bleeding hands with him. I turned to Tony to protest again, and he put his hands up giving me the I-don't-want-to-hear-it look.

"I think some of the POWs we brought back are pretty banged up, Rob. Why don't you get upstairs and see if you can't help patch some of them up. No use wasting your supplies down here...I don't think these guys will be around for long."

Sensing my hesitation, Dave chimed in as well.

"You don't need to see this, Doc. I've seen the way this ends, and it ain't pretty. After he lost his brother, well, he got a little dark. He leaves the body parts on the objectives to kill the enemies' morale."

I heard a new set of screams and heavy thud of the battle axe falling on a wooden table from the second room, and realized I would probably be able to do more good somewhere else.

"Alright, let me know if any of these guys need saving. I'll be upstairs."

"Roger," Dave replied, obviously not enjoying being a part of what he knew was in store.

Back upstairs, I checked into the team room to ask where I was needed. I ran into Bulldog first who said, "It seems our guys weren't treated too well in the camps, and the other medics are pretty overwhelmed with all the new people we brought in. Can you have a look at Corey and Tattoo to make sure they're ok?"

"Roger, sir!" I replied, hesitating and trying to think of a way to bring up what was going on downstairs with the battle axe.

"What's up, Rob?" Bulldog asked, sensing that I had something else to say.

"I'm not quite sure how to say this, sir, but I think you should go check in on The Major. It's getting a little rough down there."

"He has his way of doing things, just as we do, Rob. I'm not going to step on his toes and hope that he would offer me the same respect if we were on his turf right now."

"Yes, sir, I'll go see to our guys," I answered, not wanting to beat a dead horse at the moment.

I was splinting a pair of broken fingers when the chainsaw started. I didn't quite recognize it at first, but once the engine screamed and the blade bit into human flesh and bone I knew exactly what was going on.

I walked down the stairs into the team room at the same time The Major was walking up the other set of stairs into the team room, and as we both moved into the room from opposite sides, I was a bit surprised by what I saw, even though I knew what to expect.

His uniform was painted red with blood like a butcher who just finished preparing a fresh load, and the expression on his face was as blank as a clean sheet of paper.

"Everything alright, Major?" Bulldog asked as he walked in.

"Great. Just great," The Major replied. "I've got another mission for us, get your men together."

"Wait a second, another mission when?"

"There's a re-supply going out to some of the enemy locations tonight. We took out most of their air assets, so it's going to be a ground delivery. You guys want to make up for the stuff you lost when you left the first compound?"

Bulldog shot a glance at Josh, who responded with a shrug and said, "Well, we do need to refit food, supplies, and ammo after the last few days. Where is this supply route?"

The Major made his way to the map on the wall and immediately started plotting the route, leaving a central logistics hub in Denver and coming out to multiple locations over the next twenty-four hours.

"Remember, Russia never evolved past the big 'blue vs red' war planning, so they didn't follow our lead into small unit tactics when we went to Afghanistan and Iraq. They still work with large units and do things in large numbers, so their re-supply is one huge convoy leaving their central logistics hub and hitting several bases on the same trip."

"Like a big, slow, dumb animal!" laughed Klint.

"Exactly. But don't feel so superior - the Taliban did the same thing to us in our initial convoys in Afghanistan. It was only as a response to their attacks that we changed the way we conduct re-supply and logistics lines, so we'll see if these guys change their ways after   what we do to them tonight."

"What exactly do you propose?" asked Bulldog.

"Well our friends downstairs told me they'll be leaving Denver at sundown tonight to get as much of a cover of darkness as possible. If we hit them before they make their first re-supply, we'll have our pick of ammo and supplies, so I say we take them out before they get past Castle Rock, about thirty miles south of Denver."

"Okay," sounded Chris.

"So we take all the trucks, stop the convoy, and grab everything we can carry. What do we do with the personnel? We can't keep bringing POWs back here - we're already out of room with the three from last night."

"Oh those three?" answered The Major with a smirk. "I wouldn't worry about those three - they've already checked out of the hotel. Their rooms are ready for new guests, but I don't plan on any of their guys making it out of this one alive."

Chris, Bulldog, Josh and Tony each shared a quick glance.

"We've got to roll out in a few hours if we're going to do this. Are you guys in?" asked The Major.

"Let me talk with my leadership. Give us ten, I'll come find you as soon as we make a decision," replied Bulldog.

The Major looked around the room for a second, turned and walked out without a word, followed by the remainder of his team.

"What do you think?" Bulldog asked, looking around at the rest of us. "Should we do it?"

"Honestly, I don't know if he really gives a damn about supplies or just wants more baddies to carve up like a turkey," I replied.

"At ease on that garbage," answered Chris.

"Regardless of his intentions, he is right; we lost a lot of our supplies in the raid and we need more of just about everything, especially with the civilians we brought back last night."

"Then it's settled; even though we have The Major's guys with us on this one, we need every swinging Richard out there so we can carry everything possible. Ray, how much can we carry as far as vehicles are concerned?"

"Well, sir," Ray answered, "we've got the original trucks, HUMVEE, Bradley, and flatbed we got from Taylor.

We used the five-ton as an IED, so that one's out, but we procured another supply truck from the raid last night, so we're about even."

"Good. You guys know what to do then, let's get ready to roll in a few hours. Start getting your gear together. Recon element out the door in thirty minutes."

I could tell that we were starting to get careless as soon as I walked out of the team room.

The first mission that we went on was planned and executed with the same precision and attention to detail as we had on every mission we performed in the decade or so we had known each other.

Now we were kicking out a recon element without even a solid plan, just some basic grid coordinates of the route we were attacking and where we wanted to hit them. I silently said a prayer as the recon team sped out of the front gates on their motorcycles, hoping that the sense I had about this one was just a bad feeling and nothing more.

There remained about three hours until sundown, which meant we had to be on the road in an hour to make sure we gave ourselves enough time to get to our location, link up with the recon guys, get into position and hit the convoy as it came into our sights.

Going back to search for my family to spend some time together I quickly realized we hadn't even taken the time to unpack or get anything settled.

After being blown out of the last base, we had been on the move non-stop, and I hadn't even seen my kids since we left for the POW mission.

I found my way to our new room to find Robert sitting on the floor by himself, reading a book.

"Hey, buddy!" I said.

"Daddy!" he yelled, dropping his book and turning around to run into my arms.

"I missed you, daddy."

"I missed you too, buddy, but I told you daddy always comes home."

"Are you home for good now?"

"No, I just wanted to come and say hello. Daddy has to go back to work again tonight."

His little face dropped and he looked down with the news that I had to leave again.

It broke my heart to be away from him at any time, but I knew that his life depended on us not only being able to stay one step ahead of the enemy, but to be adequately supplied with ammo in case they found us - and food in case they didn't.

"Tell Avery that I love her too, buddy. It's your job to look after her again while I'm gone tonight. Can you do that?"

"Yes, dad," he said sheepishly.

"Hey, buddy, that's a very serious job, and I have to trust you to take care of your sister while I'm gone, or daddy won't be able to do his job because he'll be worried about you the whole time. Will you be able to be a big boy and take care of her?"

"Yes, daddy!" he replied, a little more upbeat this time.

"Great, buddy. I love you, and I'll be back later tonight. Daddy always comes back."

"Okay, daddy, I wuv you too."

Robert Patrick Lewis

Before I could put him down, he wrapped his arms around my neck and patted me on the back, as I patted the back of his head and held him close.

I didn't know if we'd ever be able to go back to the days of me coming home from work, cooking them dinner, giving them a bath and reading bedtime stories, but I sure hoped so. I left war to start a family, and now my family was right in the middle of it.

I was happy to see the commo circle when I walked out to the trucks. We were cutting a lot of corners on this mission, but at least we were keeping some of the normal routines.

Almost everyone was going out on this one, and with the addition of The Major's team, it made for a pretty big crowd.

We were setting this one up as a textbook ambush. We had an area along the route that would allow us to use the terrain to our advantage and emplace most of our force on high ground to initiate, while The Major and his team stayed down low to procure supplies from the trucks after we neutralized the drivers.

The recon team was comprised of Jason, J-Lo, Ray and Griz and had been in position for a little over an hour by the time we arrived, about a half-mile up the road from where we were to set into place.

They had eyes on the route and would let us know when the convoy was coming, how many trucks they saw, what type of vehicles, how many soldiers, what types of weapons and anything else we'd need to know. They also brought a few sniper rifles with them to pick off anyone they could at the back of the convoy while we unleashed hell.

Next in line was our heavy weapons team, which I always thought was the most fun. This was comprised of myself, Josh, Chris and Chad, and we were the ones bringing the pain.

We had two M240 heavy machine guns, a Barrett .50 caliber sniper rifle that shot a round the size of your hand, and an M249 SAW that would all be used to turn the convoy vehicles into smoking wreckage, helping us to avoid hitting any of the cargo.

The final section of our group would have typically been the main assault force, but as we had The Major's fifteen men to take care of that, we outfitted Klint and Buckeye with M79 "thump guns," handheld grenade launchers that could be used to rain down single shot M203 rounds (essentially grenades) on the convoy.

The best part about setting up in a traditional ambush was that the recon would let us know when we had to be ready, which gave us a good chance to shoot the breeze or take a much-needed nap until it was game time.

A lot of the conventional military leaders don't especially like Green Berets because they don't think we take anything seriously.

They are only right in the respect that any time we get to screw around with each other, we do - but only because, in reality, we take our jobs so seriously that we need a little time to settle down and make light of the situation from time to time.

Josh, Chris, Chad and I immediately set to task after getting in place and making sure our weapons were loaded and ready, and that we had plenty of backup ammo around to reload.

Although the time would have been better used for the naps which we all needed, we chose to use it to make fun of each other, and while talking trash didn't alleviate our fatigue, it sure was good for the soul to have a laugh with the guys.

We heard Griz's voice come over the radio just as Josh was pulling something out of his pants that none of us wanted to see, and all joking immediately stopped.

Each of us picked up our respective weapons and moved our aim to the road, preparing to send every enemy soldier who passed below us to their maker.

Griz called in the men, weapons and equipment, and let us know that the convoy was moving around forty-five miles an hour, so they should be to us pretty quickly. I chose my spot on the road that would be my starting point of fire and prepared for the action.

Waiting for the enemy to start moving into my sight, I realized it had been a bit too long since Griz's call and I hadn't seen the convoy yet. A minute had gone by, which doesn't sound like a huge expanse of time but is a lifetime when your life depends on it.

Griz's voice came back to life through the Peltor headsets over each of our ears.

"The convoy stopped."

"What do you mean the convoy stopped?" The Major replied through clenched teeth.

"I mean they stopped, sir. No clue what they're doing, but the whole convoy came to a stop."

"Let's just light them up right here," chimed in Ray from the recon position.

"Negative!" said Bulldog.

"Ray, is there any way they spotted your claymores?"

"No way, sir," answered Ray.

"Those things are hidden under the dirt on the side of the mountain. I've got remote detonators so there aren't any wires, and they're still about 200 meters from them anyway, so there's no way they saw them."

"We've got movement, sir," said Griz.

"It looks like they've got dismounts coming to check out the area."

"What the hell do you mean dismounts?" The Major silently screamed into the radio.

"Sir, it looks like they have two squads of dismounts getting in formation to walk the route. Be prepared, they're coming your way."

"Don't you worry," answered The Major, "We're ready for the bastards. Look alive, boys."

I looked down to the road and watched as the Infantry-types walked right through the kill zone, through the sights of my machine gun, and on down the road.

"Hold your fire, men. If we let loose, we'll scare the convoy and lose the entire point of this mission. Let them do their thing, get back in the trucks and then we'll light them up."

Just as the dismounted soldiers walked towards the edge of my firing lane and started getting close to The Major and his men, I heard The Major come alive on the radio.

"Screw this. Get some, men!"

The next thing I saw was The Major run up the embankment on the side of the road, bring his arm back and throw his entire body forward like a pitcher in the World Series.

The whir of a black battle axe flew through the air toward the dismounted soldiers, and as the point man in their formation met the receiving end of The Major's battle axe square in his chest and began to fly backwards, The Major already had his rifle up taking down the rest of the squad.

The remainder of their team followed his lead up the embankment, taking down all of the dismounted soldiers before they could return a single shot. Not knowing what just happened, Josh and I stole a glance at each other.

"Stop the convoy," Bulldog yelled into his radio. "I don't care how you do it, but stop that damn convoy from getting away!"

The enormous military tires screeched and the stench of burnt rubber filled our nostrils as the convoy tried to reverse its direction as quickly as possible.

I followed Josh's lead and picked up my machine gun to run to get a better shot, and as soon as we were in position, we started laying down fire.

There was no way we could get the entire convoy, but at least we could get the last few trucks (what had originally been the lead vehicles) and anything they had on them.

As soon as we had a half dozen trucks neutralized, I looked down to the road to see The Major walking toward the smoking vehicles, rifle slung across his back, battle axe in hand, dripping with blood and looking for his next victim.

"That crazy bastard," Josh said, incredulously.

"Yeah, well thank God that crazy bastard is on our side," I laughed.

"For now," answered Josh.

"I don't think Bulldog is going to be too happy with this one."

CHAPTER 11

A GLIMMER OF HOPE

I hopped out of the Bradley and made my way towards the team house to see the guys standing around outside. Buckeye stopped me as I reached for the door.

"Not quite yet, Bro," he said, shaking his head from side to side.

The muffled voice of a heated argument echoed from inside, and I already knew who the parties were.

Josh had been right on the money, and although I couldn't hear the words coming out of Bulldog's mouth on the other side of the door, I was pretty sure I knew the gist of it.

I heard the yelling getting louder and louder followed by the loud crash of something being thrown against the wall, and then silence.

We looked around at each other outside, wondering if the silence meant they had actually done each other in, when the tone changed completely.

"Chad, Matty, Griz! Get the hell in here!" came Bulldog's thunderous order from inside.

The three men summoned ran past the group as quickly as they could, with the enormous Chad almost knocking down the door in his haste.

The rest of us followed in suit, and we immediately knew what had stolen their attention upon entering the room.

The HAM radio, which normally sat quietly in its corner, was now laying on the ground with an overturned chair against it and had sprung to life, emitting a voice with a southern drawl reading off numbers and letters in the military phonetic alphabet.

"*Whiskey. Tree. Hotel. Five. Alpha. Nine.*"

Chad immediately took a knee and started writing down the message.

After the last number, a song began playing that brought a smile to my face. The rest of the team looked around confused, but to me the tune carried me right back home.

"It's '*The Eyes of Texas Are Upon You*'," I said out loud.

All men turned to me, puzzled, as I smiled, bopped my head and said, "You know, the University of Texas spirit song."

No recognition was shown in any of the faces around the room, so I began to sing.

"*The eyes of Texas are upon you, all the live long days...*"

"Seriously, Rob?!" Bulldog barked at me.

"I'm not messing with you, sir. That's the spirit song for UT."

"So what the hell is that supposed to mean?"

"Sir, I just know the song, but if you want me to guess, I'd guess this means that whoever sent this message is in Texas. Or a Longhorn fan."

As the song reached its end, the numbers and letters started again.

"*Hotel. One. Alpha. Seven. Echo. Papa. Tree. Delta. Two.*"

"Ok, Echos and intel guys, figure out what the hell this means. Everyone else out, let's give these guys some peace and quiet."

Bulldog ushered us all out of the team room, and although I was pretty curious to figure out what in the heck was going on, I knew I'd do more harm than good by taking up space and not contributing in there.

We made our way back to the trucks and started going through the containers of supplies we recovered from the enemy convoy.

The first thing that took me by surprise was the mixture of boxes, some with Russian Cyrillic writing, some with Arabic, and others with Chinese writing.

I glanced over at Klint, who stood next to me in the back of the truck looking through the containers.

"You ever see anything like this?"

"What do you mean?" he asked.

"I mean with all the different armies' gear put together. Even when we were fighting directly with the Brits and Aussies, we never collocated all of our stuff like this."

"Yeah, I've never seen that before. But if we're known for anything in war it's absolute waste. It's actually not a bad idea to put everything together. Whose trucks were they on?

"I'm pretty sure all the vehicles were Russian."

"I wonder how they agreed to split everything up in the end." Klint stopped rummaging and stood up to ponder that one after he said it.

"I mean, this isn't just about a grudge...this has to be about resources. So I wonder, at the highest levels, how exactly they agreed to divvy everything up."

"That's a good one." I stood up myself and began to ponder. "Well Russia already has the natural gas and energy market cornered on that side of the world. I wonder if they would want ours, or if China said it was theirs since Russia has their own deals with Iran."

Klint laughed a bit.

"Well, we owe China a hell of a lot more than anyone else, so maybe that's the deciding factor."

"It's probably who kills the most Yankee scum," chimed in Bryan from the front of the truck bed.

"Well, that's a bummer," laughed Klint.

Just as we all took a moment to reflect, a call came out from the team room.

"Guys, get your asses in here!" yelled Chad.

A few moments later, we were all seated in the team room around Bulldog and The Major, who stood at the center, holding Chad's notebook.

"Who wants to go to Texas?" The Major announced as he searched the group for volunteers.

"Come again, Sir?" asked Klint.

"Chad, why don't you explain this one to them?" Bulldog commanded.

Chad stood up and took his notebook back, then began.

"It seems we stumbled upon another group of barrel-chested freedom fighters much like ourselves who are crushing enemy souls down south, boys."

"Wait a second," interrupted Ray. "What do you mean stumbled upon?"

"Well, I guess I should start by saying that the HAM radio isn't exactly any of our strongest suits, and we honestly didn't expect to get much out of it. But when the radio was, uh, nudged earlier, it knocked one of the settings out and picked up a message loop that we completely missed."

The Major cut Chad short.

"Why don't you skip to the part where you tell everyone what the message means there, high-speed?"

"Yes, sir. Well the message took us a second to figure out, but it's the same code we all learned in SERE school."

Chad found nothing around the room but blank faces.

"Am I seriously the only one who remembers the code methodology they taught us in SERE school?"

More blank faces.

"You guys should really learn to pay attention. Basically, this loop is coming from another group of a National Guard Special Forces unit out of Dallas and some other Texas natives who fell back to their homes and have been defending in place there. It sounds like they've got their hands full of enemy, pouring across the Mexican border and trying to dock at ports in Houston right now."

"So what does that mean?" asked Buckeye from the crowd.

"It means, who wants to go to Texas dumbass!" shouted The Major.

Bulldog shot The Major a glance and started with an explanation of his own.

"It means we have some decisions to make. We're not going to just up and leave this place and try to transport our families all the way down to Texas through enemy-controlled territory."

The heads in the crowd nodded in approval as Bulldog paused for effect.

"But if our main objective is to take back control of our country, we can't just let our boys get overrun along the border down south."

Having heard enough, I raised my hand and spoke up.

"I'll go."

"Well that's a given, Rob" Josh laughed. "You honestly didn't get a choice. As the only native Texan on the team, you were going to be volun-told so you could be the tour guide."

Buckeye and The Major scanned around the room looking for other volunteers, and J-Lo spoke up before anyone else could.

"How many men do they have? How many do they need?"

"That's what we've got to figure out," answered Josh.

We all knew what that meant, and as we had done multiple times before, we began to spread around the room to go into our planning phase.

As easy as it would have been to just ask who wanted to go, we needed to use a much more methodical way of deciding.

It was not only important to determine who we would be sending down south to get a much more decisive view of what was going on around the country, but also who would be staying in Colorado to protect our compound and, most importantly, our families.

We knew that we would need to take at least two of every skill set so we could have an operational team going on the trip, but still leave enough behind to man the defense perimeter and be an effective force in Colorado.

The problem with having so many Alpha males in one place is that we knew what this mission would entail, and although we each knew just how important it was to stay behind and protect what we had, everyone in the room wanted the toughest mission available. After a half hour or so of having all names written on the whiteboard at the front of the team room, Corey walked up to the board and erased everyone's names, quickly re-writing in two separate columns:

Going	Staying
Rob	Adam
Klint	Jason
J-Lo	Corey
Josh	Chris
Ray	Bulldog
Buckeye	Taylor
Griz	John
Tony	Mike
Bryan	Chad
Tex	Matty
The Major	Tattoo
Dave	

"It's pretty simple." He turned around and exclaimed after writing the last name.

"Except for Rob, the team guys with kids stay, everyone without kids goes. This gives us two of every skill set minus the Echo, but I think you guys can handle that."

Corey looked around the room for confirmation as Bulldog stepped up, took a second glance and turned to all of us.

"Everyone ok with this?"

"Wait a minute," spoke up Tony from the back.

"Why are only two people from The Major's team going?"

"We're the only ones without kids" The Major responded quickly with a shrug.

Looking around the room again, Bulldog repeated his question.

"Everyone ok with this?"

Seeing a room of heads nodding up and down in approval, he gave the verdict.

"Ok, let's get moving. We need to divvy up trucks and equipment, figure out a route plan, commo plan, phase lines and an escape & evade plan for these guys in case they get into trouble."

Bulldog turned and singled me out of the crowd.

"Rob, we don't know how long this mission is going to be, or what comes after it, but we need you on this as the only person who knows his way around that big state of yours. Go get some family time...we'll get you when we need you."

I walked back to the family area to get some much-needed time with my kids. The past few days were so busy and crazy I had barely even seen them, and they let me know it the second I entered the room.

"Daddy!" Robert yelled as I walked in, immediately leaving the game he was playing with Chris' wife and kids and running full speed into my arms, followed quickly by little Avery.

As I picked one up in each arm, and felt their little arms wrap around and squeeze my neck, I was reminded of exactly why we were fighting so hard for what we believed in.

Guys like us, extreme A-type personalities who made it into Special Forces, possessed a few major qualities in common, and they weren't always the character traits one would expect.

Sure, we each possessed an extremely high tolerance for pain, testosterone and motivation that was off the charts, and an ability to utilize deductive reasoning and planning more effectively and efficiently than most guys.

But one of the down sides of all those traits was that we had a tendency to get so focused on the mission at hand, we lost focus on everything else.

It was like God gave us this gift to conquer the world, but as a price for this gift he required that we utilize it to its fullest, and make sure we didn't squander it.

And as a reminder life has a cruel sense of humor, every Special Forces guy I ever met possessed another quality which seemed to be issued right along with the Green Beret: the biggest heart and most undying love for children one could ever imagine.

For some reason, we Green Berets just couldn't seem to make it work with our significant others. It was commonplace for combat-hardened Special Forces guys to have a string of ex-wives due to our personalities.

But to observe the same barrel-chested, bullet-wound ridden and fearless soldier around his children would make anyone's heart melt immediately.

I tightly squeezed my two armfuls of everything I loved as strongly as I could, taking a brief pause to smell their hair, full of the pheromones that reminded the animal part of me they were in fact my progeny (as if I needed it), and kissing each one of them on their soft-skinned
foreheads for as extended a time as I could without making them curious.

I knelt down on my knees to put them down and remain on their level. I wanted to be as close to them as possible for as long as I could.

Once their feet hit the ground neither one hesitated, both grabbing my hand and pulling me towards the throng of kids they had been playing with.

Somehow Sarah, managed to bring enough supplies to set up arts and crafts time with all of the kids, and both Robert and Avery brought surprises for me.

Avery was the first to announce her gift; at two years old she couldn't say much more (intelligible, at least) than "Daddy!" and point, but the piece of paper with scribbled lines and a few pieces of colored yarn glued to it still warmed my heart.

"Daddy! Daddy, Avery, Guh Guh!" she exclaimed, pointing to different scribbled lines representing herself, me, and her guh guh (Mandarin for "brother").

"Wow, that's beautiful, Avery! Thank you!" I exclaimed loudly, not just grandstanding but feeling touched they thought of me.

Giving me a big, proud smile, she wrapped her little arms around my neck and squeezed with everything she had.

Obviously jealous to not be involved in the family hug, Robert quickly joined suit and we made a Lewis dog pile in the middle of the room.

Not knowing how long we had together before I needed to leave, I decided to take the kids for a walk around the compound to show them where everything was, but mostly just to spend some time actively doing something so I wouldn't get misty-eyed sitting around, looking at them and thinking about how much I'd miss them while I was gone.

It was just another of many instances where if you sat down and thought about it too much, your head would spin. I left my Brothers, the Army, and Special Forces to start a family and go to medical school, as their mother made it obvious she didn't ever want to be married and have kids with a Green Beret who could be called away for weeks at a time at the drop of a hat, without being able to say where I'd be going or what I'd be doing.

Five years later, after massive amounts of money, time and hard work, I had everything I left that life behind for: a family who I loved more than anything in the world, my medical degree and a promising future as an orthopedic surgeon. And after all that, been called back to war anyway.

It just cemented several theories I always pondered over on life and destiny.

As the saying goes, *"We make plans and God laughs."* We can make plans all day long to do whatever we want to do or think is in our best interest, but at the end of the day, it's the man upstairs who calls the shots - and if you pick one he doesn't like, get ready for a change.

I also firmly believed certain souls were created for certain paths, occupations and professions. With this I don't mean an accountant is always an accountant in every life, a lawyer is always a lawyer and so on, but I think certain life paths are re-lived by certain souls because, well, they can only be done by those souls.

I always firmly believed after my time in the Army and Special Forces that warriors were warriors for time immemorial, and that while my scars and memories were from the battlefields of Iraq and Afghanistan, my Brothers and I had been fighting alongside one another since the dawn of human existence, and possibly even before that in the pre-man battles in heaven.

Life and the Universe had given me just enough time to walk away from my warrior-soul to get the knowledge I needed to further myself and knock out another much-needed accomplishment. But as soon as it thought I was ready, it brought me right back to where I belonged.

As I walked through the tall grass around the compound with Robert on my shoulders and Avery in my arms, I pondered how in the world I could communicate that to my kids.

At two years old, Avery was far too young to even understand what I was saying, and even though Robert may understand the language, at four years old he was far too young to understand the meaning.

Knowing that it was my job as a father to impart this knowledge to them, I made a mental note that it would be a travesty for something to happen to me without being able to pass my fatherly wisdom to them, so I made a promise to myself, and to them, to begin writing down everything that happened so they would know my story.

We were spending time together in the garden, I explaining the different fruit and vegetable plants to Robert as Avery tried to sneakily steal cherry tomatoes and stuff them in her mouth before I could see, when Buckeye joined us.

He was Robert's godfather, resulting not only from our time spent as roommates in Germany, but also because I knew if anything ever happened to me, he would be the best dad I could possibly imagine for the kids in my stead.

Not only was he one of the most intelligent, physically strong and tough men I had ever known, but he also had an extremely gentle personality and a sense of compassion that was hard to find outside of a Buddhist monastery.

I spied him out of the corner of my eye before the kids did, and he put a finger to his lips in the sign of silence as he crept up behind Avery, picked her up under her arms and threw her up in the air, twisting her around so that she was looking down upon him from the apex of her flight.

Seeing it was Uncle Chad, she burst out laughing with a mouthful of tomato and greeted him with a big hug when she landed in his arms. Robert immediately lost interest in the eggplants I was teaching him how to care for and ran to Uncle Chad to envelop him in a tiny hug of his own.

Reaching down and picking Robert up with his other arm, Uncle Chad shot me a beaming grin. He took a second to kiss each of them on the forehead, but his grin faded away when he looked me in the eyes.

"Bulldog's ready for us. He said to take a few more minutes to bring them back to the group and tell them you'll be back to say goodbye, but it's almost time to start suiting up."

A silent nod was all I could send back his way, and with that he handed Avery back over to me and turned to start walking. The lump in my throat and emptiness in my heart just served to remind me why you never want those you love around you in a combat zone.

Besides the danger, fear and worry, just having to say goodbye to those people you love every day, knowing there was a better than average chance you'd never see them again, took a toll on your soul and was something I'd never wish on my worst enemy.

After dropping the kids back with Bulldog's wife and making our way into the team room, I could see by the maps, writing on the board and nervous energy from the guys that we were just about ready to move.

On the board next to the table of who would be going and staying was a list of the equipment going, and who was carrying what. It was quickly obvious the vehicles we were driving were chosen for speed and ability to move with a low profile rather than security, which made a lot of sense.

We'd be going way outside of what we knew on this trip, and although it would have been comforting to have armor and the big guns on each of our trucks, if the twelve guys we were taking encountered anything much larger than a company of enemy no amount of armor or weapons would do us much good.

The route was pretty simple; there was a lot of distance between our destination, Austin, and us, and with no real intel as to how effective our Brothers down south had been at keeping the enemy at bay, we didn't have any idea of how safe the highways would be.

We'd essentially have to use our standard operating procedure of using the Ravens as scouts ahead of our convoy, hope the enemy didn't have satellites or planes overhead to watch the highways, and stay on our feet the entire trip.

If we pushed it straight through we could make the drive in about ten hours, but knowing we needed to be cautious, I estimated fifteen to twenty would be more realistic.

The Texas group seemed pretty well organized, with their Command and Control element located in Austin and their main fighting forces near the borders in El Paso, Houston and San Antonio, where any large enemy units would have to pass through due to the infrastructure and highways.

While this wouldn't be the first trip I'd ever made using this route, having gone back to visit my old undergraduate college stomping grounds in Austin while stationed in Colorado, this would be the first time I wasn't taking a leisurely stroll, stopping at multitudes of gas stations for the trademark BBQ and kolaches that I reminisced about from the first day I left Texas after college on my way to Infantry basic training.

I studied the map intently, trying to remember everything I could about my previous trips, where we could utilize the landscape for any protection, cover and security, what would be good places to stop to fill up the trucks with gas and not be seen, and most importantly, where I would set up an ambush if I were the enemy guarding that highway.

As I was the only one with real firsthand knowledge of the route, it was up to me to set up the phase lines, dividing up the drive as evenly as possible and giving time estimates of how long it would take us to hit each, so the guys at home in Colorado would know when to expect us to call in, and when to know something had happened if they hadn't heard from us.

The first leg of the trip out of Colorado would be pretty simple.

We knew that after taking out the landing strips at DIA, the enemy had lost their ability to bring in any more heavy armor or troops in Colorado, and with the chaos we'd caused up to this point they were probably spending more time on damage control than manning the highways going out of town.

It was the movement from Amarillo to Austin that gave me the most concern. That route would take us perilously close to both Oklahoma City and Dallas, each of which had major airports, large city centers and massive populations that would be prime targets for the enemy generals who had been planning the invasion.

Although we wouldn't be going through those cities, their proximity to Interstate 27 and Interstate 20 had me worried. I believed that once we hit Highway 183 to make the final leg of the trip from Brownwood to Austin we'd be home free - but there was a lot of ground to cover before that.

I thought about possible friendly forces whose battlespace we'd be passing through; I knew that the guys we were traveling to find came from a Special Forces National Guard unit out of Dallas, so I hoped they had caused havoc in their own backyard, possibly even being smart enough to take out the Dallas/Fort Worth airport as we had with DIA in Denver.

Once we hit Highway 183, we'd be passing right by Killeen, home to Fort Hood, one of the largest Army base in the United States.

Not only was Fort Hood huge but it was home to the 1st Cavalry Division, 504th Battlefield Surveillance Brigade and the 69th Air Defense Artillery Brigade, giving me hope they had some major firepower to fight the good fight and keep enemy forces out of the area.

I divided our drive into four phase lines, not quite equal but using extremely significant points along our route.

Our first call would come once we passed through the Colorado state border with New Mexico, the second one when we passed through Amarillo, the third once we made it through Abilene, and our fourth and final call would come once we were safely in Austin and linked up with the other freedom fighters.

Once our phase lines were disseminated, radio frequencies locked in to the radios, gear packed, food stored, plans briefed, re-briefed and finalized again, it was time to get a move on and see what life had in store for us next.

I may have been the only father going on the trip, but many of the other guys had significant others to say their goodbyes to, so we were given a final hour to spend some quality time with them before setting out.

When I made my way back to the living area, I found Bulldog's wife reading, surrounded by a dozen tiny bodies lying on their blankets taking a nap.

Rather than wake Avery and Robert and try to explain what their daddy's next job entailed, I took a moment to write a quick note for them to keep until I returned.

Robert and Avery,

I want you to know that I love you more than anything in the world, and that everything I do, I do for you.

Daddy has to go and meet some friends to help us and make sure that we can keep you two safe, and I promise I'll be back as soon as I can. I want you both to be good listeners and be brave until I get home.

Robert, I want you to be my brave little knight and take care of your sister until Daddy comes home. I love you two and I'll see you soon.

Love,
Dad

After finishing the note, I folded it neatly in half, handed it to Bulldog's wife and made my way to the piece of floor my kids were sleeping on.

Laying down as quietly as I could, I put Robert on my right side and Avery in my left, nestling their little sleeping heads in my arms, thanking God for giving me these little gifts who exemplified everything I cherished in the world and gave me my sense of purpose.

I fell into a dreamless sleep almost immediately, only to be awakened by a tugging at my boot.

Looking up I saw Buckeye, and as soon as he saw my eyes open, he motioned it was time to go. I kissed each of my precious angels on the forehead, smelled their hair one last time and gave a nod to Bulldog's wife as Uncle Chad knelt down and kissed them both as well.

Part of me wished I could just lay there forever with my kids, being the loving father who spends every second of every day loving, cherishing, teaching and playing with them.
But the other part of me knew I had to show my love in a different way.

I was, after all, a sheepdog, and it was not only my job to love and cherish them, but I was one of the few put on this earth to protect them - and it was time for me to continue that solemn duty.

CHAPTER 12

PEOPLE'S ARMY OF PINELAND

The drive stayed rough and we were on edge the entire sixteen hours it took to reach Austin, but we arrived in one piece. A few of us wanted to stop and explore Dallas and Killen - snoop around and try to get an idea of what was going on in that area, but The Major wasn't having any of it.

He understood that just as we knew the lay of the land in Colorado, our best information would come from linking up with the teams who had been fighting in Texas.

They would be able to give us the details of what was happening in their area, much better than we would ever determine from driving the streets aimlessly.

Even though the message we encountered on the HAM radio was given in code, the authors of that communication had been cautious enough to not give their specific location.

While Chad had been able to crack most of the code and figure out the Texas headquarters were located in Austin, there had been a series of numbers repeating in a loop at the end, which left him completely dumbfounded.

"1, 2, 3, 4, 5, 6, 7, 8, 9, 10.
1, 4, 9, 16, 25, 36, 49, 64, 81, 100.
3, 5, 7, 9, 11, 13, 15, 17, 19.

3, 5, 7, 9."

The moment Chad recited the long string of numbers and repeated the loop, the message took me immediately back to my days of studies, bringing vividly to mind moments of learning and teachings from the past.

I realized then what it was.

But knowing it would take far too long to explain to the guys, I had to ask them to take it on faith that I had solved the code and knew exactly where we needed to go.

The first thing that struck me once we reached the Austin city limits was just how normal everything seemed.

Downtown Denver had resembled the apocalypse with abandoned storefronts and burned out cars and trucks littering the streets, and nobody driving or walking around except for us and the enemy troops.

Austin, on the other hand, seemed like it was almost business as usual, save for significantly lighter traffic than I remembered.

Looking around the city from the highway, I didn't see any significant damage, civilian cars were driving around the streets and even people moving about on the sidewalks with no sign of enemy troops anywhere.

I felt like I was dreaming as we passed the University of Texas football practice stadium on my right and saw players actually out on the field. As we exited Martin Luther King Boulevard and drove by some of my favorite haunts from college, the students walking to class acted like it was just another day for Austin.

It was only as we turned left on Congress Avenue and viewed the state capitol that anything appeared out of place. The normally open and inviting building had been fortified to an astounding level - complete with air defense artillery tanks, guns, guards, barbed wire and roving patrols.

A quick right on 18th Street - a stone's throw away from the capitol building - and our three-truck convoy came to a stop at our destination: the Scottish Rite Temple in Austin.

I hadn't been a Freemason while in college, so my only visits to the Temple had been casually driving by to take pictures and have a look while on vacations. Even so, I noticed a few modifications had been made to the normally unassuming building.

The building itself, erected in 1881 (when Scottish Rite Masonry came to Texas), only ever had three windows visible from the street, so there hadn't been any real need for significant fortification, but sandbags were piled high on the front lawn and a fortified concrete hallway had been emplaced leading to the entrances on the North and East sides of the building, with armed guards at each entrance.

Pulling around to the east side of the building to enter the parking lot, we were stopped by another set of armed guards in front of an enormous iron cattle gate blocking our way. The men looked curiously at our trucks, back to us, and approached the lead vehicle which I was driving.

"Can I help you?" the first guard asked.

I turned to The Major in the passenger seat, who shrugged and pointed at me.

"The is your show, Rob. I don't know what kind of hocus pocus or handshake you need to give these guys - just get us inside to figure out what the hell is going on here."

I looked back at the guard and tried to formulate how in the world to explain how we got there.

"Uh, we heard a transmission on our HAM radio in Colorado."

Without a word he took a step backward and pulled out his handheld radio, saying something into it I couldn't quite understand. Moments later, a tall man wearing an Army uniform and a big black cowboy hat emerged from the eastern doorway, walking toward the guard with the radio.

A nod in our direction led the tall man to our vehicle, and when he reached my window, he put his hand up to rest it on the doorframe and peeked his tall head in to get a better view of the occupants of our truck.

"So I hear ya'll got our message," he announced in a loud and thick Texas drawl.

"Roger," I replied, still a little dumbfounded by what exactly was going on.

"Well, that's great! Glad to have you boys here. So which one o' ya'll figured out how to find us? I mean, most people woulda probably stopped up the street at the capitol."

"That would be me," I answered, trying to figure out exactly who this guy was and why he looked so familiar.

"Well then, Brother, there's something we need to do. How's about you step out for a second and meet me on the Five Points of Fellowship? We can't be letting every convoy of heavily armed fellas we get coming around into our little establishment here - I'm sure you understand."

I put one hand on the door handle to open as I turned to The Major for a nod of permission.

"Rob. Seriously. I don't know what the hell you guys are talking about, so just do whatever you gotta do there, high-speed."

Figuring that was as much of a go-ahead I was ever going to get from The Major, I opened the door and stepped out into the hot Texas sun.

Getting a closer view of our greeter, I could see the insignia of a full bird Colonel rank on his chest, broad shoulders and chin at about my nose height that made me feel a bit insignificant in the presence of this giant.

As I tried to figure out how I was going to accomplish this with a man almost twice my size, he stuck out his hand, and as soon as I accepted with my grip he pulled me in, wrapped his arms around me and whispered an age old charge into my ear, and my reply proved that we were in fact, Brethren.

Once our physical and verbal exchanges were complete, he pushed me back with enormous hands on each shoulder, took a moment to look me up and down, got a huge grin on his face and pulled me back into his chest for a bear hug.

"Boy, it sure is great to see you guys. I had a hunch I knew who you were as soon as you arrived, but you know, we never can be too sure. We've heard about the good work you boys have been doing up North, but that's about all I can say before we get inside and into the SCIF [Secretive Compartmentalized Information Facility]."

He took a step back, motioned to the guards to let us through and turned back to me.

"Oh, and where are my manners? My name's Jim, and it's a pleasure to meet you boys. Park the trucks here in the lot, so they'll be safe while you're inside, and we'll go in and get you some hot coffee so we can have ourselves a chat."

As Jim turned around and walked back towards the entrance, the guys in the truck started in on me.

"Rob, what the hell was that?" asked Ray from the backseat.

"Dude." I replied in my best don't-bother-asking tone of voice.

"Uh, no. You're not getting off that easily," The Major chimed in. "What the hell was that, Rob?"

"Well, sir," I replied, "I could tell you, but then I'd have to kill you."

"Fair enough. I'm not dying today, especially not for trying to learn some handshake," he replied with a chuckle.

As each of the trucks parked, its passengers began to pile out into the sunlight and stretch their legs. After a brief moment of getting reacquainted with being up on our feet instead of glued to our seats, we made our way towards Jim.

"Nice to be back home in Texas, ain't it, Rob?" he asked me.

"Excuse me?" I asked.

"It doesn't matter how long you've been gone, Brother Lewis, Texas is always home to a true Texan."

"How do you know my name? I never told you who I was."

"We'll get to that inside. Nonetheless, welcome home."

The giant of a man looked over my shoulder to find everyone assembled and turned to lead us into the building.

After Jim punched in a sequence of numbers on a keypad and pressed his thumb on the outside of a scanner, the door buzzed and he pulled it open.

The guard at the entrance put a hand out to stop me and said, "You'll need to leave your weapons here; no weapons inside with unauthorized personnel."

"Take it easy there, killer," Jim said with a smile. "These boys are about as authorized as it gets, and if I know anything about them, they ain't putting their weapons down until they're dead."

The guard gave me a quick once-over and stepped aside as we followed Jim into the building.

He led us down a large hallway bustling with activity and men walking from room to room in uniform, carrying folders and documents as if they were en route to meetings.

In the middle of the hallway, Jim turned and opened a tall set of doors, looked around to make sure we were still following, and led us into an enormous theatre room.

Inside, we saw that what was once a theatre used for concerts and plays (complete with stadium seating, a stage, lights and even red carpet) had now been transformed into a strategic control center.

The room was lined with workstations, computers, flat screen TVs showing video feeds, surveillance and even an Internet Relay Chat [IRC] screen like we used downrange.

Walking us halfway into the room, Jim turned his massive shoulders around to face us and make sure we were all within hearing range before he started.

"Welcome to the war room, boys. This is where we take our country back."

Each of us scanned the room and marveled at the bustling activity that was buzzing all around us. We had been confined to a team room with a HAM radio, wondering what was going on in the rest of the country while the scene here was reminiscent of the Special Operations Command control centers we all spent many hours working out of and receiving intelligence briefs in Baghdad and Kabul.

"What the...?" The Major started, but was immediately cut off with a finger to the lips from Jim.

"Any questions you boys have will most likely need to be answered in the SCIF. Follow me."

And with that, Jim began walking with his giant paces and led us up the stairs onto the stage, past the large briefing boards and flat screen TVs, behind a curtain and through a narrow hallway to a door, guarded by several armed men.

"Now, I'm sorry, but you know the drill. No cellphones, radios, weapons, cameras or anything besides you and your swinging Richards inside this room. Kindly leave anything in your pockets here in the lockers, and these nice gentlemen will keep them safe for you," Jim said, pointing towards a row of plain gray lockers set up on either side of the door.

Seeing we had each emptied the contents of our pockets and placed our weapons in the racks and lockers, Jim turned to face the door, punched a code into a keypad next to it, pressed his thumb onto a small pad and pressed his face into another small rectangular box next to the door.

After a few seconds, the door buzzed, the lock clicked, and Jim opened the door. He stepped inside, motioning for us to follow him. We walked into a much smaller, institutionally gray room, lined with battle maps and computer terminals with uniformed men sitting at the computers, reading and typing.

Jim moved to the far side of the room, pulled out a chair from one of the terminals and took a seat, facing us. He motioned to the other chairs in the room, and as we sat in a circle around him, he said,   "Now I'm sure you boys have loads of questions to ask, but I've got a few of my own. After that, I'll give you a brief on the current situation, and then you can feel free to ask me any questions that are still lingering and haven't been answered. Sound fair?"

We each nodded in approval, still awestruck at the entire situation.

"First and foremost, I understand you boys are operating in the area surrounding Fort Carson, and we saw that you laid a pretty significant hit on DIA and managed to take out the runways. Good job, but how in the world did you pull that one off without coordinating with our unit there at DIA?"

"Wait a minute," Josh started in. "That was one of your units?"

"My unit isn't exactly accurate, and you're to hold your questions until the end of this thing. So your question leads me to believe you don't know anything about the teams we have there at DIA?"

We looked around at each other and shook our heads.

"Ok, next question. We know you guys took a load of civilians from the Lodge in Denver on your way home from that hit. Are they alright?"

"We lost one adult and a significant amount of the kids when our compound was attacked," answered Josh.

"Which adult?" asked Jim, leaning forward and becoming very interested in the answer.

"Jacob," replied Tex in his thick Texas accent from the back, who had been among the group we brought in with Jacob. "We lost Jacob when they hit the house with all the kids in it."

Jim nodded briefly, pausing for a moment and not saying anything while he moved his head slightly in affirmation.

"Anyone else?"

Each of us in the circle around him shook our heads as he absorbed our response and let out a heavy sigh, as if he anticipated our answer but hoped he was wrong.

"And the rest of your group, they made it safely to your secondary compound? Any indications the enemy knows where they're currently located?"

"We don't have any reason to believe they know where our secondary location is," Josh answered.

Jim silently pondered this for a moment and continued to pensively look around our circle.

"Ok, then let's get started. The invasion may have officially begun less than a month ago, but in reality this thing has been in the works for years. In hindsight, some of you probably put the pieces together on what led to this whole thing starting, but there were those of us who saw the chess pieces moving into place a long time ago. Hence, our ability to have such an infrastructure ready to go when it happened. I assume you guys had a feeling this was going to happen as well, or else you wouldn't have built the compound and been able to organize so quickly on your own."

He glanced around the room again, ensuring we were each paying attention and following what he was saying.

"Perhaps I should start at the very beginning. If you haven't figured this out yet, a lot of this was an inside job."

As he spoke this damning sentence he paused and reviewed our faces, this time looking every one of us in the eyes, ensuring that we were grasping the importance of what he had just said.

"Our country was envisioned as the greatest social experiment known to mankind, a place where freedom of religion, expression and from tyranny would reign supreme over all, giving each of us the right and ability to create our own destiny and forge whatever future we could for ourselves, our country and our coming generations. But unfortunately, not everyone could abide by those virtues, and certain greedy and pugnacious elements soon found their way into some of the most highly-esteemed and powerful positions of our leadership."

Jim stood and walked to a wall, upon which hung portraits of many of the US presidents and politicians who had been Freemasons and were adorned in their Masonic regalia, starting with George Washington.

"We created and forged this country, her Constitution, Bill of Rights and Declaration of Independence to create a shining beacon of greatness for the world to see, but with a true sense of democracy, we chose not to influence the outcome of who would lead the charge of this magnificent social experiment. Over time, those who we hoped would continue to shape the landscape for the betterment of mankind over their own self-interests were replaced by career politicians and megalomaniacs seeking nothing more than wealth and power."

Speaking the last few lines with utter disgust in his voice, Jim began to pace around the room.

"Over the past several decades, the pestilence of greed has overtaken this majestic land, and politician after politician has put his own self-interests first, made selfish choices for re-election over the greater good, and destroyed everything we had built. Not only did they set up what was quickly becoming our means for self-destruction, but in the last few years when it was readily apparent there was no way out of the hole they had dug us into, those same politicians began to negotiate with our enemies in a way of saving their own skin when this happened."

"Wait a minute," chimed in Dave. "What do you mean negotiate with our enemies?"

"Your questions come at the end, but that was where I was going next anyway," answered Jim.

"When it became obvious that our currency and economy were doomed, certain politicians began to bargain with those forces we're currently fighting - mainly China, Russia and Iran - to ensure specific steps were taken to make their takeover of the United States of America as seamless and painless for them as possible."

He paused and allowed that to sink in for a moment as he continued pacing.

"They rescinded the 2nd Amendment and began to disarm the American people - the right given to us by the creators of this impressive social experiment to combat a greedy and corrupt government who would dare do something of this magnitude.

From the beginning of time, we masons have sworn to protect this country and her people against all corruption, greed and evil, and have always taken positions in government to ensure that. Some of us were given the heads-up of what was coming, and began to plan accordingly.

By the time we received any word, it was far too late for our small numbers to come out and do anything, as the politicians who were acting against the greater good of our nation would have simply locked us up in jail with no trial or ability to defend ourselves. All we could do was plan and wait."

Jim walked to a map of Texas on the wall, and pointed to Austin with his index finger before continuing.

"Thankfully, Texas has never fully trusted the politicians in Washington and revered our rights and ability to protect our people above all, so when the President tried to enact a repeal of the 2nd Amendment, the Governor told all law enforcement officials that if they attempted to take weapons away from any Texas citizens, they would be locked away in prisons themselves."

He pointed to several other locations on the map of Texas, showing us which cities housed large military bases.

"The Federal government then instituted The Base Realignment and Closing [BRAC] Commission, threatening to close all federally-funded military bases on Texas soil, essentially leaving us open for the slaughter when the enemy tanks started rolling. But lucky for us, most of those dim-witted and weak politicians had never served a day of military duty in their lives, and didn't understand just how much of a headache that would become. So Texans stayed armed, and we still had our bases the day the invasion began."

With this, Jim turned back to the group and said with a huge smile, "And that, my friends, is why they say *'Don't Mess with Texas.'*"

He next walked over to a larger map, riddled with red and blue thumbtacks and military symbols denoting friendly and enemy units, sizes and makeup.

"On a larger scale, unfortunately, the rest of the country didn't see things the same way. The Yankees up North and on the East

Coast - and your hippies on the West Coast, Rob - were quick to give up their 2nd Amendment rights as soon as Big Brother asked, leaving themselves unarmed. The BRAC commission succeeded in drawing down most of the military presence in those areas as well, so when it was time for the invasion to come, the enemy rolled right on in without much of a fight."

He pointed to the northern border of Canada.

"It all started with small pockets of enemy fighters, mainly Iranian Al-Quds and Hezbollah terror cells coming in from the northern border with Canada. They've been here for years, mostly in the North preparing for the sign to start creating chaos in the first few days of the invasion."

He then pointed to the West Coast, focusing on Southern California and upper Washington State.

"Concurrently, the Russians were sending KGB and Spetznaz in along the West Coast with the same ultimate plan; while the politicians were disarming our people, they were using the black market to stockpile weapons from people like the California Senator who was the only one to get caught smuggling arms to our enemies, but that didn't slow the rest down one bit."

Next he pointed to the East Coast.

"The infiltration of the East Coast was led by fighters from the Middle East and North Africa, and we have everything from Al-Qaeda Arabian Peninsula (AQAP) to ISIS and Al-Shabab there to cause havoc on their own."

He turned back from the map and towards us again.

"All the while, state-sponsored Chinese and Russian hackers have been working for the past decade to learn how to take down our energy grid and communication network. They figured it out finally, thanks to some leaked documents from our own politicians bargaining for their personal seat at the dinner table. And the rest is history.

Day one, the communications and energy grid went down, and the terror cells caused chaos. The big boys, Russia and China, started flying their troops and sailing their troop transport ships as soon as the grid was down, and here we are."

He took a deep breath, shrugged and looked around at us again.

"Now, are there any questions?"

We took a moment to let everything sink in, some of us looking a bit dazed with blank expressions on our faces, while others felt the anger rising within. It was The Major who first spoke up.

"Didn't you say something about hot coffee earlier?"

Jim bellowed with laughter, doubled over on his knees and took a minute to respond as he wiped the tears from his eyes.

"Man, that's why I love being around SF guys. It's been awhile since I've had a good laugh."

He tapped one of the men at the computer next to him on the shoulder.

"Can you please go get these men some hot coffee?"

He turned back to us and opened up the floor for questions again as soon as the door was closed.

"Anything else?"

I raised my hand and stood up out of my seat, unable to sit still any longer.

"Yes, Rob?"

"I've got two questions for you, sir. First, how in the world did you know who I was without me introducing myself, and second, who the hell is that unit at DIA? You said we have a team there, but they're not yours?"

"Ah, yes, both very good questions. First, you boys may have spent your life as good operators and Green Berets, trying to stay off the radar, never putting anything incriminating out there in social media or the public light, but rest assured that every one of you is on a list."

He pointed a finger directly at me.

"Especially you, Doctor Robert Patrick Lewis, former Green Beret and Brother of the 32nd Degree in the Scottish Rite of Freemasonry. You're on quite a few lists."

He shrugged his shoulders and continued.

"When we knew this was all going down, we began preparing and planning in more ways than just stockpiling ammo and food. We worked to determine who would be our greatest assets around the country. Special Operations Command has known your plans for quite some time, and thankfully there are many other groups like yours, fighting the good fight all around the country."

He smiled with the last statement as he pointed to the map of the United States again as a reminder.

"Ok," I replied, "but now for the second question. Who the hell was that at DIA?"

"That," he said before pausing, "that's going to take a little bit longer to explain. Maybe you should sit back down."

I took my seat and listened intently as Jim started again.

"This, my friends, is one time that an ever-growing and overreaching government worked in our favor."

Jim slowly lowered into his chair, showing some pain in his back and knees as he laboriously pulled his chair around and sat down with a grunt.

"You see, somebody got the great idea in the eighties to start making huge military complexes underground, just in case we ever actually came to nuclear blows with Russia."

"But weren't those in Washington DC for the government to run the country?" J-Lo asked.

"The first one was, but once the Joint Chiefs saw how well that went, they realized how strategically important it would be to keep other bases scattered throughout the country."
"But why Colorado? Why Denver?" asked Ray.

"They're strategically located, everywhere they would give military and defense importance," answered Jim.

"Not only to us, but to anyone who ever tried to invade us, as you boys saw."

"You're still not telling us who exactly is there," I interjected. "Masons? Military?"

"You're correct on both accounts."

"But how in the world would something that big stay hidden? I mean that must have cost quite a bit of money. How did the politicians who sold out our country not give the enemy that info as well?" I asked. "It seemed like they were just as surprised as us when soldiers started coming up from underground."

"You boys should know as good as anyone about compartmentalization of Top Secret information. Just because you have Top Secret clearance doesn't mean they tell you who killed JFK and where Jimmy Hoffa is buried the second you're cleared."

"Yeah, I get it, but something of that magnitude?"

"Well, if you think of the big picture, the black budget for the Department of Defense alone has topped $50 billion a year for the past decade, so in the grand scheme of things, it really wasn't even that big a piece of the pie. Think about it, boys...that's billion - with a 'B'. You can buy a lot with that kind of money, especially when the labor is supplied by government agencies."

I couldn't believe what I was hearing.

"The whole point of compartmentalization is to keep things on a need to know basis," Jim continued, matter-of-factly. "And fortunately, the first General put in charge of these bases was not only a true patriot, but of course a Mason, who chose the inner circle to command these projects wisely and made sure access to anyone who knew about them was extremely tightly controlled."

"So you're saying that all of these bases are full of Masons?" I asked again.

"Not entirely, but mostly. The clearance required to even know about one of those bases is well above top secret, and while we initially tried to ensure everyone involved was a Mason, the size of the project grew to a level that couldn't be sustained with Brothers alone. A security clearance which would get you into Delta force or the CIA wouldn't even get you in the front door there."

"So why even let the enemy land and set up shop there? I mean those guys had enough troops to have stopped it cold at the beginning; why even let it go that far?" asked Dave.

"Morale, my friend, it was all about morale. Sure we could have stopped it at the very beginning, but you boys have always been a bit sheltered in Special Forces, keeping to yourselves and not worrying too much about the general Army. But imagine the stories being told back in Russia and China now that the body bags are coming home."

"How did you know it worked? I mean, what if they just send twice as many troops to take back the airport?" asked Buckeye.

"Well, why don't you answer that one son? Have you boys seen a single plane in the sky since that mission? You dealt the bad guys a serious blow! Now the enemy on the ground in Colorado is stuck with no way to get home, no reinforcements, and no supplies. That and the airport in St. Louis were their keys to the Midwest, and they never made it into St. Louis."

"So it sounds like everything is going in our favor then, right?" asked Tony.

"Not so much," answered Jim. "Even though Denver was their only major landing spot in the Midwest, they've successfully crossed every border except ours here in Texas. We've got some pretty serious fighting around the clock all across the Mexican border and at our ports where they're trying to land ships, so we can't count our chickens just yet."

"How is the border holding up?" asked The Major.

"Well the military bases in Texas have always been stacked pretty well. We've got quite a bit of artillery and combat aviation out of Fort Bliss in El Paso, Air Force and Army bases in San Antonio, Navy and Coast Guard all along the southern part of the state on the Gulf of Mexico. The rest of the country had a lot of trouble recalling their National Guard units once the communication grid went down, but we had enough active duty units here to be pretty effective without having to call people in."

"So you're saying you think you have it pretty well covered?" asked Josh.

"Well, boys, I could tell you, or I could show you. How about I take you on a little trip to the front lines of World War III?"

To be continued in *The Pact Book II: Battle Hymn of the Republic*...

ABOUT THE AUTHOR

Robert Patrick Lewis is a Special Forces combat veteran of Iraq and Afghanistan-turned author, entrepreneur, MBA, marketing professional and investor.

Robert served as an 18D (Special Forces Medic) and during his time in 10th Special Forces Group (Airborne) he deployed to Afghanistan, Iraq twice and North Africa as well as multiple other training missions around the globe, with a final deployment to Afghanistan as a military contractor.

He left the Army with a Purple Heart for wounds received in Afghanistan, the Special Forces tab, the Combat Infantry Badge, Bronze Star, Army Commendation Medal, NATO non-article 5, Iraq campaign ribbon with cluster, Afghanistan campaign ribbon and many other awards for his service.

After his time in uniform was over Robert set out to write about his experiences. He has three published books including his non-fiction military memoir *Love Me When I'm Gone: the true story of life, love and loss for a Green Beret in Post-9/11 war* and the first two books of his fictional trilogy, *The Pact* and *The Pact Book II: Battle Hymn of the Republic*.

He has been featured on national programs such as Fox News, The Dennis Miller Show, The Adam Carolla Show, The Herman Cain Show and writes frequent articles for Heroes Media Group.

Robert has two children, two stepchildren and is engaged to the love of his life (and editor) Natalie Pimentel. He writes from his homes in Los Angeles and Dallas.

CPSIA information can be obtained
at www.ICGtesting.com
Printed in the USA
LVHW091356140419
614125LV00003B/1073/P

9 780985 940461